OFF THE WALL

A collection of

Fantastical Fiction,

Fractured Fairy Tales,

& Friendly Phantoms

By Gary Breezeel

OFF THE WALL - FANTASTICAL FICTION, FRACTURED FAIRY TALES, AND FRIENDLY PHANTOMS

First edition. December 15, 2024.

Copyright © 2024 Gary Breezeel.

ISBN: 979-8230231615

Written by Gary Breezeel.

Table of Contents

Many thanks to the members of the Scribes critique group of American Christian Fiction Writers for the many improvements they helped me make to the stories and to Kim Vernon Rodgers for her invaluable assistance in putting this book together.

I also want to thank fellow members of White County Creative Writers for their encouragement and support.

Cover: Kim Vernon Rodgers, Canva.com, and Pixabay.com

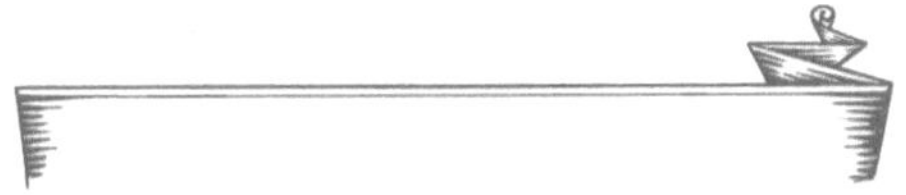

PART I
FURRY FUN

Stories featuring animals with human-like characteristics

Weather Burrow

Rusty fumed as he watched the latest hype on the large-screen TV at his favorite restaurant. Why did everyone make such a huge production out of Groundhog Day and that worthless Punxsutawney Phil? *Humans can be so gullible.*

What a phony. Did some overgrown ground squirrel control the weather? Not on your life.

Could he even predict it? Uh, *no.*

The confounded furball did nothing but hang around in his burrow until a so-called scientist from the National Weather Service reached in and dragged him out to see, or not see, his shadow. Whichever fit their predetermined notions of whether or not spring might come early this year.

Big Deal.

Rusty glanced up as his waitress approached. He always requested a table in Rosalie's section. She was so cute.

With a flourish, she set his plate before him. "One extra-large portion of Buffalo Grass Fricassee. We at Prairie Dogs R Us aim to please. Particularly our *special* customers." She shot him a coy smile.

He pushed his heavy glasses up his nose. "Looks delicious. Thanks, Rosalie." One of these days, he would have to summon up the courage to ask her out. He turned his attention to his food as she returned to the kitchen. The flavor exploded on his taste buds, heavenly as always. He had to exercise every ounce of control he could muster to keep from shoveling it in.

A cocky, too-familiar voice sounded behind him. "Well, well. Look who's here. What brings you out of your hidey-hole, Nerdly?" Biff, his high school nemesis, *would* have to show up. "Did you get the crazy notion you're fit to mix with your betters, which is everybody in Prairie Dog City?"

The largest youth in the class, Biff had served as captain of all the sports teams, which meant all the females for miles around wanted to date him. No wonder he exhibited an air of superiority toward the small, bookish student with thick glasses he'd nicknamed Nerdly Four-Eyes. By all accounts, the former jock hadn't matured in the fifteen years since graduation.

Rusty acted as if he were searching behind Biff. "Where's your entourage? Did they wise up to you, at last?"

"Very funny. Ha, ha. I'm dating Cathy Comely, this month's centerfold in *Prairie Playdog Magazine*. She's at a photoshoot." He thrust his forepaws onto his hips. "Say, Nerdly, I'm surprised you haven't starved to death. Must be hard to support yourself while closeted in your burrow day and night."

Rusty raised a paw to hide a smirk. Contrary to his old enemy's expectations, he made an excellent living in his "hidey-hole." He had numerous inventions in production and operated a successful computer consulting firm with hundreds of clients, both rodent and human. He refocused on his meal. Perhaps Doofus would get the message and go away.

Biff grunted, then sneered. "There's something strange about you, Nerdly."

Mouth dry and with tingling toes, Rusty grabbed his latest — and greatest? — invention, almost a year in the making. Would it work? Time for the final test. He stepped out of the secret, high-tech lab hidden beneath his luxury apartment, locked the steel security door, and made his way to the surface. He peeked out and rotated 360 degrees. No predators in sight.

He hopped onto the ground and touched a button on the device he held. A frigid north wind swept across the prairie. *Looking good.*

When he pressed another button, clouds rolled in within seconds, and rain fell.

Rusty jumped up and down. "I've done it." Now, he needed to figure out what to do with his invention.

O n the last day of January, Rusty hitched a ride for the final leg of his journey on a flatbed semi. When the rig pulled into a truck stop off I-80 near DuBois, Pennsylvania, he hopped off and scuttled into a nearby pasture. Butterflies fluttered in his stomach. Less than thirty miles from Punxsutawney. Close enough for his purposes. Time to put his plan into action.

He pulled out an apparatus that resembled a prairie dog-sized garage door opener, moved a dial to *Slow Build,* a second to *Epicenter 28 Miles*, and clicked *Activate.* That should do it. Clouds would roll in today, followed by heavy snowfall early on February 1. By daylight, the blizzard would paralyze traffic in Punxsutawney and for twenty miles around. Prior to dawn of the next day, two feet of snow would bury the area and disrupt power for hours, if not days.

He smirked and gave a smug laugh. So much for the Groundhog Day media circus. This would expose Punxsutawney Phil as a fraud, once and for all.

He glanced at his phone. Two o'clock. Plenty of time to take a nap and still hop a westbound semi and escape "the scene of the crime" before traffic slowed to a halt. With any luck, he would make his way back to South Dakota in time to watch the debacle on TV. He snickered.

B ecause the return trip took longer than anticipated, Rusty didn't reach Prairie Dog City until the morning of the second, past nine a.m. Eastern Standard Time. The fun should already have begun.

He rushed into his apartment, fired up his home theater system, turned on his television, and selected The Weather Channel. An unfamiliar reporter bit the inside of her cheek as she stared into the camera. "Um...we expected our regular anchors to broadcast live today from Punxsutawney, Pennsylvania." Her eyes darted from side to side, and her hands twisted together. "However, a surprise winter storm...has paralyzed portions of West Central Pennsylvania and disrupted...communication from the region. We'll connect with Joel and Crystal as soon as possible. In the meantime, enjoy this report on the beaches of sunny South Florida."

Rusty laughed out loud. Everything was developing according to plan. Later, he would take the next step.

At seven p.m., he switched on the super-transmitter he'd developed to override the signals of all the alphabet networks and major cable news channels. He had bounced his signal off numerous towers around the world to make it well-nigh impossible to trace. *Heh-heh.* Plus, he'd placed the lights to show nothing but his shadow on TV screens as he spoke into one of his inventions, a device to translate his words from Prairie Dog into English.

"Good evening, ladies and gentlemen. I've interrupted your regular programming to make an announcement of importance. A blizzard not predicted by the National Weather Service has struck parts of Pennsylvania. Forecasters failed to anticipate this storm because it did not occur out of natural weather patterns. I have learned how to control meteorological phenomena and used this knowledge to produce this event for one purpose — to expose Punxsutawney Phil for the fraud he is!

"That phony can't predict the weather. He doesn't even exit his den on his own. Some yo-yo from the weather bureau does it for him. And yet, television networks spend significant broadcast time covering the Groundhog Day foolishness to find out if he sees his shadow. What a bunch of hogwash!

"I've proved my point. Southern breezes will blow warm air into the area after midnight tonight, and sunny skies tomorrow will melt the snow. Punxsutawney will return to normal within thirty-six hours. Thank you and goodnight."

Rusty smiled as he clicked the off button. *Mission accomplished.*

Three days later, Rusty pushed away from his kitchen table with a groan. There were only so many ways to prepare buffalo grass. He needed variety in his diet. Perhaps tumble grass for a change. Besides, he'd been closeted in his lab too long. Time spent outside while he foraged for the treat would provide a pleasant diversion, not to mention fresh air.

The elevator carried him to the surface, and he popped out onto the ground. Hmm, where might he find a stand of tumble grass? If his memory served him well, there was a sandy area in the pasture about a quarter-mile north. He set off in that direction.

Sure enough, a twenty-foot square patch of the plant he sought grew in the exact place he remembered. Far more than he needed.

He opened the sack he'd brought and stuffed it with the delectable vegetation.

Rusty's head snapped up. What was causing that buzzing sound? A swarm of angry bees? His heart raced as he whirled around and searched the sky.

At last, he spotted the source—a drone, not furious insects. He breathed a sigh of relief, then scratched his temple. How odd. What was an unmanned aircraft doing out here where humans seldom ventured?

The craft went into a dive in his direction. Machine gun fire burst forth and tracked toward him.

He dropped the sack and bolted to one side. Good thing he was small and shifty. Still, he couldn't avoid the confounded contraption forever.

The drone turned and zeroed in on him again.

He changed course and raced for home as fast as he could go. Seconds later, projectiles again struck inches away.

With no way to outrun the dastardly device, he needed someplace to hide.

As the craft circled to make another pass, Rusty spotted an abandoned ground squirrel burrow twenty feet to his right. He sprinted toward it and flung himself into it a fraction of a second before bullets strafed the opening.

He took several deep breaths. Safe. For the moment.

After ten minutes, he peeped outside. *Here comes the blasted drone again.*

He ducked out of the line of fire and hunkered down inside. What now? Those things could stay in the air for hours.

Why not keep hidden until dark? If the particular model didn't have infrared or heat-detection capabilities, he might make it back tonight. Thank goodness he had set out on his foraging expedition after dinner. Not too long to wait.

An hour later, Rusty plopped onto his couch. *Whew.* He'd made it with no sign of his mechanical nemesis, but without a doubt, his enemies planned to relaunch it and resume the search in the morning.

Unless he wanted to remain a prisoner in his own home forever, he would have to work out how to deal with the aerial weapon. He didn't expect to sleep much that night.

The next afternoon, a makeshift periscope rose out of the main entrance to Prairie Dog City, Rusty at the other end. He scanned the airspace. As expected, the unmanned device circled about a hundred yards away.

He adjusted the settings on his weather controller and popped out of the hole. When the cursed craft turned in his direction, he pointed the instrument and pushed a button. Lightning flashed out of a cloudless sky. A bolt struck the drone, which shuddered and then plummeted to earth.

With a grin, he scurried to where the apparatus lay. Not too badly burned. He studied the wrecked mechanism. *Just as I thought. Too small for military grade.* A six-prop commercial model with a machine pistol attached. Amateur hour.

Who ordered a hit on me? He rubbed his chin.

After his coup on Groundhog Day, Phil held a grudge against him, no doubt. Nobody liked to be exposed as a fool, but the oversized rodent lacked the intelligence to pull off something like this. Besides, where would he find the money to purchase a drone or to put out a contract? Which left the weather bureau. Rusty had humiliated them, as well.

Not good! With unlimited resources, the U.S. government could pursue him with relentless determination until they accomplished their purpose. Which meant he'd have to devise a plan to make them stop.

No time like the present to begin. He pivoted and scampered toward his lab.

Rusty stepped into the open outside his homeplace for the first time after a week of nonstop work. He set his new, improved weather control device to the geographic coordinates for Silver Spring, Maryland, faced east, and pressed the activate button. Then he raced inside and tuned his TV to The Weather Channel.

After fifteen minutes, a newscaster interrupted the program with a special report. "In a shocking incident, eight inches of marble-sized hail has fallen on National Weather Service headquarters. Incredibly, the hailstones struck an area limited to a two-hundred-yard radius around the facility. An agency spokesman declined comment on the strange occurrence."

Rusty laughed. That ought to grab their attention. He picked up his modified satphone with built-in translator and dialed the number of the National Weather Service Director.

An alto voice answered. "Director's Office, how can I help you?"

"I need to speak to the director."

"Who may I say is calling?"

"Ask him if he enjoyed today's meteorological event and desires to discuss what's next on the agenda."

"Then, you're the one who—"

"Correct. I cannot tell a lie."

"How do we know you're really—"

"Just listen." He pressed a button. A loud clap of thunder resounded through the phone. "Now, put the director on the line. At once."

"Yes, sir. Right away."

After a moment, a gruff male voice said, "This is John Ericksen. What's this about?"

"Rusty here. I want you to call off the dogs."

"I don't know what you mean."

"Cut the bull. I don't appreciate getting shot at, and I won't take it lying down, as my little demonstration a while ago should have established. I assume you don't want softball-sized hail to pummel your headquarters, so let's talk turkey."

"Although your stunt generated tons of adverse publicity, I have no knowledge of any attack on you."

"I guess you don't think I'm serious." Rusty pressed a different button. "Check outside your window. Note the golf-ball-sized hailstones. In one minute, they'll become baseball-sized... unless you come clean."

"Okay, okay. Let's assume for the moment that I ordered the drone strike."

"Yeah let's, especially since I didn't mention a drone."

"What are your terms?"

"I want two things. First, you cancel the hit you put out on me."

"Done."

"Second, you retire Punxsutawney Phil and any alternate groundhogs forever."

"I'm not sure we can do what you ask. We have loads of time and money invested in the media event. It generates considerable positive publicity for the bureau."

"Hogwash. It's all a bunch of hooey, anyhow. Besides, everybody knows your people manipulate the situation to fit what your professional meteorologists predict."

"What do we receive in return for all these concessions?"

"I agree to work for you. Use my invention to prevent, or at least mitigate, severe weather and floods, end droughts, create rain to extinguish forest fires, and the like."

"I need to bounce this off of my deputy."

"Okay, you have five minutes."

"Not enough time."

"Make it ten, but not a moment longer."

"I'll see what I can do."

In eight minutes, Ericksen came back on the line. "Deal."

"Let me confirm what we've agreed to. You cease all attempts to kill me and stop the foolishness with Punxsutawney Phil. In exchange, I work for you."

"Right, with one further stipulation. We keep this agreement between us. No leaks."

"My lips are sealed, but in case you consider reneging on our bargain, I've recorded our conversation and arranged for copies to be delivered to CNN and Fox News if anything untoward should happen to me."

"Not a problem. I assume I can reach you at this number whenever we need your services."

"Correct. So long." Rusty disconnected and blew out a deep breath. Everything had turned out all right, but he'd made a narrow escape. Nearly lost his life because of his jealousy of the attention paid to Punxsutawney Phil and letting his resentment spur him into an act of revenge. He would never misuse his technological prowess to exercise his pique again.

His stomach growled. But for now, he craved Buffalo Grass Fricassee. Served by Rosalie.

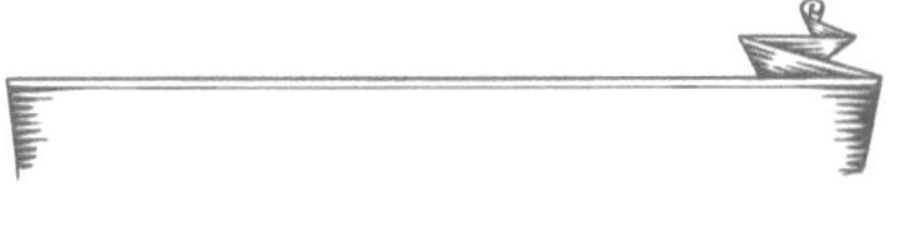

Cat-tastrophe

Thwack!

A sudden jolt knocked Captain Felix to the deck. He gathered himself and stood.

Lieutenant Sylvester glanced over his shoulder. "Sir, we've lost power, and we're careening out of control."

"Access reserve power and regain control at once."

"Aye, aye, sir. I'm attempting to bring the backup generator online as we speak."

Felix stepped across the bridge. "Dr. Mouser, The Lunar-Tuna is the ultimate spacecraft. How did we suffer damage to this extent?"

"I can't say for certain. We must have struck some sort of space debris that our sensors failed to detect."

The ship shuddered.

Felix pivoted. "What was that, Sylvester?"

"I've regained control, but we've wandered into the gravitational pull of an uncharted planet. I can't achieve enough thrust to break free."

"Can you make a smooth landing?"

"No, sir, but with luck, I can choose where we crash land."

"Okay. Give it your best efforts. How long can we remain airborne?" *Keep calm, Felix. The nine lives of your crew depend on it.*

Sylvester turned in his seat. "Thirty seconds until touchdown."

Felix touched his communicator. "This is your captain speaking. Prepare for a forced landing. Strap yourselves in and brace for impact."

Half an hour later, the chief engineer descended the ladder and shuffled toward Felix, his face downcast.

Felix snapped to attention. "That grim, Mouser? Report."

"Yes, sir. A stone pillar crushed the after portion of the spacecraft. The engine's beyond repair. We're marooned here. And what's worse, the food synthesizer's smashed."

"I guess we should look on the bright side. Although we have no way to return home to the planet Felina, the crew sustained no serious injuries, and this planet has an atmosphere not unlike our own, however bleak the landscape." Felix scanned their surroundings. Nothing but rock formations as far as a cat's eye could see.

He strode around past the ship where Tabitha, the first officer, had assembled the ship's company. "Commander, what have you learned?"

She smoothed her whiskers. "The first patrol reported moments ago. Found a claw-some spring a half-mile away near a cave large enough to provide shelter for two hundred crew members, but no sign of life."

"That means no food."

"Correct."

Over the next hour, patrols sent in the three other directions returned having spotted nothing but rocks, rocks, and more rocks.

Felix sighed. "Tabitha, we've traveled together for a long time."

"Yes, sir."

"Assemble another patrol. I think I need to check out the area myself. Perhaps, an in-person inspection will spark an idea. This is no time to pro-cat-sinate. If we don't find a way off this planet within a week, I'm paw-sitive we're doomed."

"I'll gather our tech team right away."

Exhausted, Felix dropped to a seated position. After two hours, he'd found nothing useful. Neither had inspiration struck. "Might as well catch a catnap before we start back."

The four additional members of his party stretched, yawned, and curled up at his feet.

A low growl began a distance away and increased in volume as it drew nearer. Felix rose, crept to a nearby boulder, and peeked out from behind it. The others soon joined him. When one attempted to step past him into the open, Felix extended a forepaw. "Halt, Petty Officer. Haven't you heard? 'Curiosity killed the cat.'"

The offender dropped to the ground and peeped around Felix's legs. "What is it?"

"A landing."

"Who can it be on this uncharted planet?"

Felix pointed. "Take a closer look. It has to be those mangy mutts from Pluto. Who else would build a spacecraft in the shape of a giant dog biscuit?"

The noncom stared at Felix. "A strange coincidence. I wonder what they want?"

"Us. They must have been near enough to detect our forced landing. Came here to finish us off. Let's head back before they disembark. The Commander will have set up camp near the spring by the time we return."

Later that day, Felix crept over to where Tabitha and the two other members of her patrol hunkered down behind a boulder. "Commander, what did you want?"

"Captain, I thought you'd want to see this for yourself." Her paw moved in an arch toward the rock.

With a sigh, Felix raised his head and peeked over the top. Sure enough, Captain Barf and three other curs marched past en route to the site where the Plutonian ship had landed.

Tabitha whispered, "They passed by traveling in the other direction twenty minutes ago. I overheard the leader mention a search for someone but couldn't make out who."

"Doesn't matter. We know what they're up to. Let's get back to the others. Quiet now. We don't want to alert them to our presence."

The next morning, Felix sent for Tabitha, Sylvester, and Dr. Mouser. When they arrived, he led the key team members out of earshot from the rest of the crew. "With no food available, we can't hold out for long. Since we've traveled beyond the range of our planet's communications, we have no reasonable expectation of rescue. So, we must escape this planet or perish. Our one hope is to seize the Plutonian spacecraft. Unless one of you has a better idea."

He glanced from one to another. Tabitha shook her head, but nobody spoke.

"Mouser, can you render their foreign craft operational?"

"Indubitably. How difficult can it be? A bunch of mutts created the vessel."

"Excellent. Sylvester, can you pilot it?"

"I can handle anything that flies. Besides, I agree with the good doctor. Any conveyance dogs built is bound to be rudimentary. To operate it will be like lapping a bowl of cream."

"It's settled then. Commander, select a two-cat team to observe their spacecraft. Choose those who can remain undetected, but one must be a swift runner. Have them in place prior to dawn tomorrow."

"Aye, aye, sir. What's the plan?"

"They will follow the mongrels' search party. Once they reach any of the points I have marked on this map" — he handed it to her — "the speedy one will return and report. We will need a ruse to lure as many of the remainder as possible away from their ship before we attack. I'll send a patrol close to their vessel. They won't be able to resist sending their strongest force out to capture our decoys. Any alternative suggestions?"

With a saucy grin, Tabitha spoke. "I have one. Not an alternative, but an enhancement. After the second group leaves, why not have Pandora and some of the more alluring Siamese kittens spread out blankets and sunbathe within sight on the opposite side of the vessel? To serve as a distraction for many of the pups inside."

Felix nodded. "Purr-fect, Commander. Prepare both groups. Remember, the diversionary force must convince the enemy that it's a legitimate patrol."

She saluted. "Aye, aye, sir. I'll make sure they understand the critical nature of their mission."

"Meanwhile, I'll assemble a strike force of our fiercest fighters. We *must* capture the vessel if we wish to survive. Dismissed."

Early the next morning, the raiding force moved into position and hid themselves behind boulders a short distance from the Plutonian craft.

Tabitha rushed to Felix. "The runner just reported, Captain. The canine search party has reached checkpoint C. I've briefed the distraction team. I'll lead them out in five minutes, followed by the sunbathers ten minutes later."

"You'll command the patrol yourself?"

"Yes, sir. To ensure complete success."

"Very well. Good luck, Commander."

"Thank you, sir."

Tabitha and her troops passed nearby. Soon after, a dozen well-armed canines hurried past, headed in the same direction.

Sylvester stepped out. Felix lifted his paw. "Not so fast, Lieutenant. Calm yourself. When the mutts get too far away to return in time, I'll give the order and we'll rain down on their spacecraft."

Once the sunbathers had taken their positions, Felix yelled, "Meow!" Fifty cats streamed out from behind the rocks, up the ladder, and into the enemy spacecraft. With the Dobermans on patrol and the Rottweilers in pursuit of the diversion, the remaining crew consisted mostly of lapdogs, who provided little resistance. Within moments, the felines had captured the bridge and the captain.

The lieutenant returned, along with the Alleycats under his command. Ahead of them, they pushed two dozen assorted canines with their tails between their legs. "This is the last of the captives, Captain. What shall I do with them?"

"Take all the prisoners outside. Hold them there until we have our entire ship's company on board."

"Aye, aye, sir. Come on, you worthless hounds. Down that ladder." He and his troops followed the captives out.

Soon after, Tabitha entered the bridge. "Captain, we gave our pursuers the slip a while ago. I went back to the caves and picked up the cats you left behind. Met the decoys on the way here. Sent Chief Jinx to fetch Pandora and the girls."

"Well done, Commander. Tell the lieutenant on guard detail to fire shots toward the prisoners and drive them away from the ship. Then, bring everyone onboard and retract the ladder."

She hurried to the exit.

He whirled around. "Mouser, do you have the engine ready to go?"

"Yes, sir. Easy-peasy. As I figured. Those dogs are simpletons."

"Sylvester, as soon as the hatch is secured, set a course for Earth."

"Earth, Captain? Not home?"

Felix nodded. "We need to travel to a neutral planet where we can contact our command. If we approach Felina in an enemy vessel, they may shoot us down. If I feel generous while we're on Earth, we might let Pluto know where to pick up their strays."

"Sir." As Felix about-faced, Pandora approached. "All secure."

Felix purred. "Mr. Sylvester, get us underway. When we reach home, it's catnip for everyone. My treat. We've gone boldly where no feline has gone before."

Dog Gone

" *¡Ay, caramba!* Life is so unfair." A canine with such courage, such intellect should have been born a majestic Great Dane, a sleek Doberman, or a heroic St. Bernard. But *No-o-o-o.* Fate trapped me in the body of a — *Gasp* — Chihuahua.

To make matters worse, they named me *José*. A Mexican dog called *José*, how original. Not! I suppose I ought to cut Billy some slack. One ought not expect too much of a twelve-year-old human.

Perhaps, my attitude needs work, because I don't have it too bad. Billy's dad works as chauffeur and gardener for the Chadwyck estate. Yes, *those* Chadwycks, the ones who own half the state. Billy has the freedom to roam over the whole five-acre property and takes me along. What fun.

We have the run of the place all day, but Fritz, the Chadwycks' Doberman, rules at night. That's right, a German dog named Fritz. Yet, since he's a watchdog and not a pet, perhaps, they gave his name little thought.

Nobody visits the grounds with Fritz loose. Lithe and swift, he looks and acts fierce. Like everyone else, I shivered whenever he was near. Until I got disoriented one day and found myself outside his kennel. Lucky for me, he was off duty. On the job, he's as ferocious as he appears. Otherwise, he's a pussycat.

Fritz has a lonely life — on guard duty every night and locked in a cage all day. Since that chance encounter, we've become fast friends.

And then there's Fluffy, Mrs. Chadwyck's champion Pekingese, and the love of my life. Such beauty. Such elegance and breeding. Smart, too — her intelligence rises almost to the level of mine. Yet, she scarcely deigns to acknowledge my existence. Without pedigree, I am beneath her notice. She lives in her own room, one of thirty in the big house, while I share a four-room garage apartment with Billy and his dad.

Last week, I trotted up to her near the koi pond and whispered her name. She stuck her nose in the air and turned away, but I love her, nonetheless. Perhaps, someday she will come to appreciate my unique qualities and realize I am the man — er — dog for her.

One day, when I dropped in to visit Fritz, his head drooped.

"*Mi amigo*, what is the matter? Cheer up. It is such a beautiful day."

"I have ample reason to be upset. I have failed in my job."

I growled. "What do you mean? There is no better watchdog in the city. I have heard Mr. Chadwyck himself say so."

"Not after last night. While I made my rounds, something sharp pierced my backside. I turned my head. Feathers protruded from my rump. I grabbed the awful thing in my teeth and yanked it out. Glimpsed something shiny before everything faded."

I gasped. "How terrible. What happened?"

He shook his head. "When I awoke, the sun had risen. I lay sprawled on the ground. Mr. Chadwyck and a police detective stood over me. The policeman said someone had shot me with a tranquilizer dart."

"Why did they do this?"

His head sagged lower still. "I'm sorry, my friend. They broke into the house and took Fluffy. After Mr. Chadwyck learned of this, he yelled at me and banished me to my kennel."

"Oh, no!" I struggled to draw a breath. My dear one dognapped! Who could have done this despicable deed? I panted for a moment before I spoke again. "Did they mention ransom?"

Fritz shook his head. "Not in my presence."

"I am concerned for Fluffy's safety, but all we can do for now is keep our ears open. The police will find her and bring her back." *I hope.*

"*José*, I see how you look at Fluffy. I know you care for her. It's my fault they took her. I will do anything I can to help."

"No, Fritz. You did your best. You're not invincible. You have no defense against a dart gun. I do not blame you. We will trust the authorities to save her. Meanwhile, we must remain alert. Perhaps we shall discover something we canines can do to assist in her return."

The police made no progress over the next three days, according to what Billy's dad told him at breakfast. Later, when I passed the open window of Mr. Chadwyck's study, I overheard his conversation with Mrs. Chadwyck.

"Meredith, I spoke to the dognappers by phone moments ago. They demanded half a million dollars for Fluffy's return. They'll call at midnight with instructions. If we don't comply with their demands, we'll never see Fluffy or her diamond collar again."

I gulped.

"Oh, Thorndyke, can you arrange for sufficient funds in such a short time?"

"Yes, my love. I have that much in negotiable bonds in my safe."

"Please, meet their demands. I must have my sweet Fluffy back."

"I've already agreed, dear. I'll summon Fields and have him drive me downtown to convert the securities into cash."

I breathed a sigh of relief. They planned to pay the ransom. *Gracias a Dios.* What a tragedy if those miscreants were to harm my Fluffy. *Sí*, though she ignored me, I considered her *my* Fluffy. I would find a way to earn her respect.

I dared not trust humans to make correct decisions in matters canine, but what could one such as I do in these circumstances? Over the next two hours, I devised a strategy. I waited until Billy went in for lunch. Then I visited Fritz, the first step in my ingenious plan. "*Mi amigo*, would you help me rescue Fluffy?"

"Of course. This is all my fault."

I raised a forepaw. "No more guilt trips. I must remain outside tonight to go along when they deliver the ransom. Please don't eat me by mistake when you discover me on the grounds."

"*José*, my friend, I might chew on you a little, but I'd never eat you." He gave me a doggy smirk. "Seriously, you know I will do what you ask."

"*Muchas gracias, mi amigo.*"

When Billy called me for dinner, I remained hidden. I disliked causing my human to worry, but it was unavoidable. I had to find my Fluffy.

Since canines never wear wristwatches or carry cellular phones, even a brilliant one such as I would have no way to determine when midnight drew near. So, as soon as it grew dark, and the groundskeeper released Fritz to patrol the grounds, I stepped out and waited for him.

As he approached, I scurried over to him with my plan. "*Amigo*, I shall hide behind the shrubbery beside the garage. I expect whoever delivers the ransom will take one of the cars. Once an opportunity presents itself, I will act."

"Good luck, my friend."

"*Gracias.* I'll need it." I returned to my place in back of the shrubs to wait.

After an eternity, Billy's dad descended the stairs, opened the garage door, and pulled the Bentley out into the driveway.

Soon, Mr. Chadwyck dashed out, a duffle bag in one hand. "They insisted I come alone. I won't require your services tonight, Fields. You may go."

"Yes, sir. Thank you, sir." The chauffeur nodded and stepped away.

Mr. Chadwyck set the duffle on the seat and slid under the steering wheel. I darted out, jumped into the car, and squeezed behind his seat before the door slammed shut.

Several minutes later, the vehicle stopped. When Mr. Chadwyck exited, I hopped out, too. Woodlands surrounded us. He left the duffle bag at the base of a tree painted with a fluorescent yellow X. Then he returned to the Bentley, turned it around, and drove away.

Alone in the wilderness, my eyes grew wide as I surveyed the dark, lonely forest. What could a size-challenged dog do in this situation?

Jose, focus on your strengths, not your weaknesses. But, of course. My brain, not my body, would save the day. *I must put my excellent mind to work.* Yes! When the villains picked up the ransom, I would follow them to their hideout and rescue Fluffy. Somehow.

As I reached the shelter of a nearby tree, a motorized vehicle with a loud engine approached. Moments later, an ancient, battered motor scooter zipped into the clearing. The rider extended an elongated hook, snagged the duffel bag, and reversed course.

I followed as fast as my stubby legs permitted, but lost sight of him. Still, I managed to remain within earshot until the noisy engine went silent. What *imbéciles* not to replace the defective muffler before they used the conveyance in a crime. No doubt, the authorities would soon apprehend such incompetents.

I continued along the path till I reached a glade. The scooter leaned against one side of a shack. As I crept forward, two men burst out the door. I dropped to the ground.

One culprit rushed to the rear of an SUV parked in front and raised the hatch. "Hurry! Let's get outta here."

The other rolled the scooter to the SUV. While they lifted it inside, the second man asked, "What about the dog? We promised to release her."

"Forget it. It's just a *dog*. We've got the money and the diamonds. Why should we care what happens to some mutt? Come on. Let's go."

Those blackguards, Fluffy might starve for all they cared.

As they drove out of sight, I raced to the shack. *I must reach my beloved. At once.* I ran around and around the rundown dwelling. On my third circuit, a tiny shaft of light near the ground at one side of the shanty caught my attention. I scurried to it. A rathole, perhaps. Although I was not a rodent, I wriggled inside.

I scanned the empty room. No sign of my true love. I hastened through an open doorway into a second room. She lay in one corner, head on her forepaws.

I hurried to her. *"Querida,* are you well?"

She hopped up and whirled around. In her terror, she must not have picked up my scent. *"¡José!* You came for me!"

"You know my name?"

"Of course. I am neither blind nor stupid."

"But you always act as if I'm not there."

She raised her head high. "I'm canine royalty, and you are not. A girl has to keep up appearances." She met my gaze. "Still, I *am* glad you're here. Can you help me?"

"I shall do my best." I led her to the rathole.

She thrust her head through, but her shoulders stuck. So, she wriggled back out and turned to me, with her tail drooping. "I can't get out. What will I do?"

"Do not despair, dear Fluffy. I hate to leave you here alone, but I need assistance to set you free." But how could I obtain the required help? If only humans understood dog-speak as dogs understand human-speak.

I jumped up and down. "Aha! *Mamá* always said canines have an uncanny ability to find their way home. I shall put the adage to the test. To go and bring Fritz. It is our one hope." Between my brain and his brawn, we would devise a way to save Fluffy.

She touched my face with one paw. "You can do it, *José.* I have faith in you."

"Adiós, mi amor." I shimmied through the aperture.

As the sun crested the horizon, I arrived at the estate and located Fritz before the caretaker returned him to his kennel. Between us, we dug a hole large enough to allow him to crawl under the fence.

He let me ride on his back as we raced toward the shack, although I had to hold on to his collar with my teeth to keep from falling off. With his speed, we reached it without delay, and straightaway, advanced to the rathole. If a rodent had chewed through the shanty's wall, no doubt, Fritz's powerful jaws could enlarge the opening.

"*Amigo*, I have the answer. You can pull away sufficient wood to free Fluffy."

"Step aside, *José*, I will rescue her for you."

Instead, I squeezed inside and approached my true love. "Don't worry, little one. Fritz will succeed in mere moments."

Together we watched while he gnawed and pulled and pulled and gnawed. Within the hour, he had doubled the size of the hole. Fluffy wriggled through with a good millimeter to spare.

Seconds later, I emerged behind her. She ran to me and nuzzled me. "*José*, you saved me! You're my hero!" Then, she kissed me again and again. Dog slobbers dripped off me, but I didn't mind. I was in hog — er — dog heaven.

The Chipmunk Air Force

"Hey, guys, come over here. I want to show you something." Chauncey pushed his horn-rimmed glasses up his nose while Spike and Jett trotted over to join him at the door of his lab. "Follow me. You'll want to see this. I've done it, at last." *If everything works out as planned.*

Spike's face tightened, and he raised his eyebrows. "Done what?"

"Devised a way for us chipmunks to defend our colony from predators." He led them into a huge room with a garage-type door on the far side. "Feast your eyes on these."

Jett shook his head. "Big deal. I've seen humans fly similar drones dozens of times."

"Not like mine. Although I started with two standard quad-prop drones ordered off the internet, I've modified them. Note the bubble on top near the front. It covers a cockpit where I've relocated the controls. They're now manned aircraft."

Spike's eyes brightened. "Cool."

"And though most drones can remain airborne no more than forty-five minutes, I've created an improved battery that will keep them in the air for up to three hours on a single charge."

Spike leaned forward. "Can we try them out?"

"Sure. That's why I called you in here. You two are the exact type of guys I need as test pilots. You thrive on excitement and don't mind taking a risk." A thought niggled. But *were* they suitable? They tended to be cowboy types who pushed the envelope too far for a thrill.

"Sounds like a hoot, but how will those things provide protection from our enemies?" asked Jett.

"I saved the best part for last. Note this tube underneath the body. I created a device that fires an electrical charge, a simulated lightning bolt. I've mounted one on each aircraft."

"Wow! I can't wait to go fox hunting." Spike pressed an imaginary button. "Zzzzt... *Zap!*"

"Hold on. I developed these systems for defense, not for sport. Besides, the charge lacks sufficient power to kill predators but will deliver a nasty shock and ought to stun them long enough to enable our friends and neighbors to escape. After a while, they'll learn to give chipmunks a wide berth."

Spike nodded. "I guess that's still pretty cool. When can we try them out?"

Chauncey chuckled. He figured they'd be eager. "How about now? Let's wheel them outside."

He pressed a button on the wall, which raised the door, and helped his two pilots push the former drones out into the open. Then, he explained the controls and how to use them.

Once they'd hopped into the cockpits, he handed each a set of headphones. "These will let you communicate with one another and with me."

The two closed their canopies and took off.

After they'd flown around the area for about fifteen minutes, Chauncey held a radio to his mouth. "I've prepared a series of targets in the field to your west, straw figures similar in size to foxes. I've soaked them in a substance that will emit a puff of smoke when struck by an electric current. Let's test your marksmanship."

Spike said, "Jett, I'll beat you, hands down."

"Not on your life, Dirtbag."

Spike circled, zoomed toward the first straw effigy, and fired.

Jett snickered. "You missed by a country mile. Watch me."

"Only ten feet to the left, and it was my first try. Let's see you do any better."

As Jett neared the target, fire zigzagged from his aircraft but went wide by a similar amount, but to the right.

After an hour's practice, both pilots hit about half their targets. Chauncey pressed the Talk button on his radio. "Excellent for your first outing. Time to come in."

"No way. This is too much fun. Don't you agree, Spike?"

"You bet."

"Guys, unless you want to crash, you'll land now. I anticipated your reaction and didn't give the batteries a full charge. You have two minutes left, at most."

"Aw shucks," Spike said.

"Spoilsport."

Jett and Spike zoomed around the practice range. Over the last month, they'd grown adept at maneuvering the modified drones. On cue, Jett dipped toward a target and launched a bolt. Smoke billowed upward. Another direct hit. They rarely missed anymore.

Chauncey picked up his radio. "Well done, guys. You're almost out of juice. Might as well bring them home."

A moment later, both landed on the driveway outside his lab, which now served as the hangar, and together the three pushed the aircraft inside and plugged them in to recharge.

Spike pumped his fist. "Awesome! I'm good. Not a single miss." He faced Jett. "And did you see my loop-de-loop?"

"Whoopee do. I only whiffed on one pass...because a rabbit hopped by as I was about to fire. Didn't want to blast a harmless distant cousin."

Chauncey chuckled. "Guys, guys, enough banter. You both did well. In fact, I think you're ready for a real mission." He paused and studied them. "Tomorrow, a group of our fellow colonists plans an excursion to a nearby meadow to forage for food supplies. The last time, a fox attacked and injured two chipmunks before they could reach safety. One was my nephew."

Jett stood up straighter. "What's the plan?"

Spike's paws tightened into fists. "Yeah, what do you want us to do?"

"The team expects to leave at eight a.m. You'll be airborne by five of and fly cover until they arrive at their destination. Then you'll patrol the air above for as long as they remain away from the colony. If at any time a predator approaches, you attack. Is that clear?"

Spike saluted. "Yes, sir. You can count on us."

Jett nodded. "Right. This is what we've trained for."

"Thank you. I'm proud of you both. You've made remarkable progress in a short time. Report at 7:30 tomorrow for any updates and flight prep."

"Aye, aye, sir," the two said in unison. They all but ping-ponged off the walls as they marched out the door.

Such enthusiasm. Chauncey chuckled. *Oh, to be young again.*

Both pilots awaited Chauncey outside the hangar when he arrived at 7:15. Jett smiled and licked his lips while Spike bounced on his toes. Chauncey grinned and shook his head. He'd have a hard time holding back these eager beavers.

He unlocked the door and ushered them inside. "Have a seat in my office."

The two younger chipmunks took chairs in front of Chauncey's desk and leaned forward as he seated himself. "Nothing has changed since yesterday. You still take off at 7:55 to provide cover when the foragers leave the colony."

Spike rubbed his paws together. "Aw, can't we go earlier? We want to get in the air. Perhaps look around for danger before the group comes out?"

"Not a wise move. We must make certain you retain enough battery life to protect them until they reach safety. Which means you'll need to maintain a reserve in case something goes wrong or they're delayed."

"Oh, gnats!" Spike's shoulders slumped.

"You'll do an excellent job, I'm sure. I'll keep track of what happens via the video feed from your aircraft and remain in contact by radio. Any more questions?"

The two pilots glanced at one another, but neither spoke.

"Okay, go ahead and perform your pre-flight checks."

Although both completed their examination within ten minutes, they stomped around and groused for another twenty until time to wheel their planes outside.

As the two climbed into their cockpits, Chauncey gave them a final caution. "No unnecessary hotdogging. You don't want to run out of juice too soon."

Spike rolled his eyes as he clicked his canopy in place.

The propellers burst into motion. With a buzz, each craft zoomed into the air.

With a smile, Chauncey returned to his command post inside. His pet project had gotten underway.

Moments later, he watched on video as two dozen of his fellow residents ventured out of the security of the colony. Both drones' cameras followed the foragers until they reached the meadow and spread out to search for food.

Then, Jett continued to patrol overhead, while Spike circled the area, moving outward in a spiral pattern as Chauncey had trained them. After forty-five minutes, Spike reported in. "No sign of danger."

"Excellent. Return to the meadow. Jett will assume reconnaissance."

"Roger Wilco."

Chauncey grinned. Spike must have been watching old war movies again. "Jett, did you hear my exchange with Spike?"

"Yep."

"As soon as he's in place, take over the wider recon."

"Will do."

The next hour passed without incident. As Jett flew back to join Spike in flying cover for the homeward trek, an odd shape moved on the video display from his camera.

Chauncey said, "Jett, circle around and pass over the downed tree again. I thought I spotted something."

"Okay." He made a wide turn and approached the area a second time.

Spike's camera showed rapid movement toward Jett's location.

Chauncey needed to stop him. "Spike, maintain your position. Another predator might be in the vicinity. Don't leave the group unprotected."

An audible sigh passed through the radio. "Yes, sir." His camera's motion slowed and reversed course.

Chauncey returned to the video from Jett's camera. "I was right. Fox at two o'clock."

"I see him. He just darted behind a tree."

"Hover nearby. Don't approach until he moves out into the open. He'll have to in order to stalk his prey. When he does, attack from his rear to cut off possible retreat into the woods."

"Sure thing, boss."

A couple of minutes later, the fox slipped out from his hiding place and crept across the meadow, his gaze fixed on the nearest chipmunk.

After the predator traveled about twenty yards, Chauncey shouted, "Now!"

Jett swept into motion and approached from behind. At the last second, the wily canine glanced over his shoulder. A bolt zigzagged from Jett's aircraft and struck the critter, which halted in his tracks, shook, and keeled over.

"Great job, Jett. Hang around in case he recovers and decides to cause more trouble. Spike will escort the foragers safely home."

"No problem."

After about five minutes, the fox struggled to his feet and wobbled from side to side as he slogged back into the forest.

Chauncey watched the pilots destroy one target after another. In the three weeks since Jett's coup with the fox, no predators had presented themselves during any of their missions. From comments over the last several days, the patrols had grown routine, the practice runs too easy, which with fellows like these translated to boring. A sure sign of problems in the near future.

"Say, boss." Spike's voice. "Is there any way you can make our drills more challenging? Moving targets maybe?"

"I'll see what I can do, but it may take a while."

Spike yawned. "I was afraid of that." His plane zoomed into a loop-de-loop.

Not one to be outdone, Jett buzzed the hanger, missing it by inches.

"Guys, you need to come in before you get into trouble."

Spike chortled. "Not a chance. This is the first fun we've had in weeks...Jett, are you game for a real thrill?"

"Not a good idea, fellas. You'd better land, now."

Jett said, "Nah. We've still got plenty of juice. Spike, what've you got in mind?"

"How about a dogfight?"

"Yeah, that oughtta be a hoot."

"As your commander, I insist you return to base."

Two voices shouted in unison, "No way!"

Spike sped away to the west with Jett in hot pursuit. Each plane dipped and rolled. Jett maneuvered into position behind Spike and fired, but he curled to the left at the last second and dodged the bolt.

"A lucky escape, but I'll get you next time."

"I doubt that. Soon, the shoe will be on the other foot."

Chauncey pleaded with the guys to cut it out and come back to the airfield, but the pilots continued as if he hadn't spoken.

Spike made a tight turn to the right and came up behind Jett. The chase was on.

Jett executed turns, rolled, and dived, but couldn't shake the other plane off his tail. Spike fired. The bolt struck Jett's aircraft. Smoke streamed from the motor.

"Now you've done it. I knew this would happen." Chauncey had warned them, but did they listen? Not for a moment.

The propellers slowed to a stop. His plane dropped like a stone.

Chauncey sprinted toward the field where it had fallen.

The aircraft lay on one side, its canopy popped off. Inside, Jett moaned. Blood trickled across his face, but at least he was alive.

Spike landed nearby and ran up to the crashed airplane. "Is he all right? I didn't think—"

"That's for sure. You didn't think." Chauncey pinned him with his gaze. "Or you'd have realized this was the inevitable result of a dogfight with live weapons."

A moment later, Jett's eyes fluttered open. "What happened?"

"Your...uh...friend shot you down. How are you?"

He moved all four paws. "Woozy...but otherwise okay...I think. How's my plane?"

"Irreparably damaged. I'll have to order a replacement. After this stunt, I'd scrap the entire project if it weren't so important. Now, let's get you out of there."

In the week since the crash, neither Jett nor Spike had uttered a word of complaint about practicing on stationary targets. With one airplane available, they'd had to take turns in the air but showed not a single sign of hotdogging.

Chauncey shaded his eyes and watched as Spike dived toward target after target and destroyed each with precision. Both pilots had matured and become more focused. His project might succeed, after all.

When a massive shadow passed over him, he gazed skyward. *Oh, no!* A red-tailed hawk circled overhead.

Chauncey legged it toward the hanger a hundred yards away. He'd never make it, but he had to try.

Above and behind him, a high-pitched buzzing sound fast approached. He whirled around. Spike's aircraft dipped and fired. The bolt zapped the aerial predator in mid-swoop an instant before it reached Chauncey.

The bird stopped in midair, shuddered, and dropped to the ground. It landed on its feet but stood motionless, as if dazed.

Chauncey raised the radio he still held. "Come on, let's get you down and the plane into the hangar. He'll recover soon."

Moments later, Chauncey and both pilots watched from safe inside while the raptor shook its head, looked from side to side, and flew away.

Chauncey turned to Spike. "You saved my life. Thank you."

"Just doing my job."

"You did it well, and I appreciate it."

"Why so modest?" Jett stepped closer. "You pinpointed the danger, took action, and eliminated the threat. Besides, taking down a hawk in midair is way cooler than zapping a fox on the ground."

"You two have grown a great deal and won't require as much direction in the future. I'm convinced our fellow chipmunks will remain safe from predators from now on." Chauncey slapped each of them on the back. "Well done, boys."

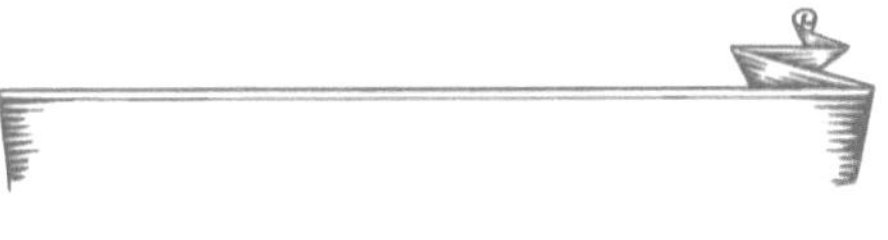

Sweet Misfortune

"Stogey, wait for me!" I raced after him as fast as my short legs allowed. Why had I chosen a bear for my best friend? Should have stuck to raccoons like myself. I sighed. Oh, well, I'd made my bed...

Arms crossed, he stopped and tapped one foot while he waited. He shifted the ever-present cigar to the other side of his mouth. When I asked him once why he never lit the things, he told me he couldn't stand smoke. Besides, he might grow careless and cause a forest fire. I didn't bother to ask why he chewed on them. The contradiction added to his...charm?

Panting, I drew to a stop in front of him.

Stogey inclined his head to stare down at me. The porkpie hat he always wore tumbled off his head, bounced off my nose, and landed at my feet.

I stooped and picked it up. As I whacked it on my flank, dust filled the air, far more than it could have acquired on the ground. I sneezed and handed it to him.

He accepted the hat and placed it atop his head. "Hurry, Zorro, you've already cost us too much time. We can't afford to miss it."

He took off at a fast walk. I churned my legs in an attempt to keep up. *Huff.* "Miss what?" *Puff.*

He glanced over one shoulder and smiled. "You'll see."

Soon, Stogey stopped behind a forsythia bush and parted the branches. I joined him and did the same. A family-size tent stood in the middle of an isolated campsite surrounded by forest. A shiny, new-looking black crew cab pickup sat off to one side. After a moment, I spotted what had captured Stogey's attention—a white-frosted birthday cake, complete with unlit candles, inside a glass carrier on the picnic table.

"Zorro, my friend, do you understand why I wanted to hurry?"

"I'm well aware of your sweet tooth, but how did you find out about the cake?"

A broad grin filled his face. "I overheard the woman tell her husband she needed to stop at the general store to buy candles."

I shook my head. Stogey put the CIA to shame when the espionage involved sweets.

He popped out from behind the bush. "Come on. They must have taken a hike before the party, but they may be back any minute."

I dashed into the meadow to join him.

When he reached the table, Stogey removed the cover and picked up the cake. "Want some?"

"You know I don't like sugary foods. Give me veggies any day."

"Of course, I do. That's what makes you such a wonderful sidekick, but I thought I would ask." He opened his mouth and stuffed in half the cake, candles and all.

I rolled my eyes. What a character. Time to get down to serious business. Where there were desserts, real food couldn't be far away. I surveyed the campsite.

Aha! An ice chest with a secure latch. Sufficient to keep out bears, but not a skilled bandit. With the dexterity common to my species, I released the catch and yanked open the lid. Jackpot! Containers brimming with carrots and lettuce, along with see-through bags of corn-on-the-cob filled one side of the cooler. Steaks, chops, and ground beef occupied the remaining space. *Thank you, Yeti.*

After I'd eaten my fill, I crammed more of the delicious veggies into a plastic bag I had emptied, as much as I could carry. Time to find my sweet-toothed friend.

A loud belch resounded behind me.

Problem solved. He reclined against a tree at the edge of the meadow and rubbed his stomach. "Ooh! I knew I ought to have removed those candles."

I raised a paw to my mouth to hide a grin. "More like you should have taken time to taste the cake instead of swallowing it in two gulps."

"Nah, I'm certain it's the wax. Must not agree with my—*burp*—digestion."

Several voices sounded nearby.

"Run, Stogey, they're coming back."

"I'm not sure I can move."

My ears perked up. "I hear engine noise, too. We'd better go."

"Owww!"

"Pardon me, folks, have you seen a bear anyplace around here?" A voice I would recognize anywhere.

Stogey leaped to his feet. "It's Ranger Jones, Zorro. Let's make tracks." He sprinted across the campsite into the woods. I dropped my bag of veggies and followed at a slower pace. The ranger wouldn't notice someone my size while searching for a bear.

Later, I caught up with said bruin in one of his regular hideouts, a cave hidden behind a waterfall. He was leaning against the wall, trying to catch his breath.

I strolled up to him. "I thought you were too sick to move."

"It's called motivation, my dear Zorro. Motivation. If that blasted ranger finds me, he'll shoot me with a tranquilizer dart and relocate me deep in the forest, far away from the tourists. Thinks I ought to eat nuts and berries like the other bears. Nuts and berries! *Bleh!* No telling how long it would take to find my way back and get my hands on a sweet treat." He shuddered. "He's got it in for me. All because I made off with a cherry pie his wife left on the windowsill to cool. How was I to know she'd baked it for him special?"

Not an overdramatic bone in his body. Yeah, right.

"That three-layer cake ought to hold you off for a while. We need to focus on the present. By the time we rest up here and let our food settle, the ranger should be long gone." I yawned and rubbed my eyes.

"Good idea, little buddy. I could use a snooze myself." Stogey stretched out on a pile of leaves and pulled his hat down over his eyes.

I awoke and pushed to my feet. Then I tiptoed to the cave entrance so I wouldn't wake my still-sleeping friend and peeked around the waterfall. Uh-oh. The sun had moved to the other side of the sky—the east. We'd slept half the day and all night. My stomach growled.

Stogey sat up with a yawn. "Terrific nap. I feel rested. Do you think the ranger will be gone by now?"

"Most likely. It's morning."

"Morning!" He rubbed his belly. "No wonder my tummy's pressing against my backbone. We'd best head out and try to find some nourishment. Like cinnamon rolls. Or doughnuts. Yum!"

I grinned. He'd never change.

"Come on, Zorro. Time's a-wasting. I hear fresh pastries calling my name." He dashed out of the cave but slowed to sidle along the narrow passage behind the waterfall, which allowed me to catch up as he stepped out into full sunlight.

"Please, slow down. I can't keep up."

"Very well, my short-legged friend, but we don't want to miss breakfast." He shortened his steps and adjusted his pace to mine, which would last about two minutes before his eagerness for sugar-laden treats motivated him to move at breakneck speed again.

Perhaps, if I engaged him in conversation, I'd distract him and prevent him from losing me in his haste. "Say, Stogey, I've never understood. Why do you call me Zorro?"

He eyed me but didn't answer right away, so I continued. "I mean, Zorro is Spanish for fox, but I'm a raccoon."

"Elementary, *amigo*, elementary. Zorro was a legendary hero in Old California. He wore a mask. You look like you're wearing a mask." He spread his arms. "Makes perfect sense."

I coughed to cover the laugh I couldn't quite suppress. Might have known. Stogey logic. Incomprehensible to a rational being.

I'd better change the subject before I lost it and broke out into a fit of uncontrollable laughter. "Where are we headed?"

"To a place where we can watch the store. They sell loads of doughnuts every morning. Let's wait until someone carries out a big box. Then we'll follow and figure out a way to grab the loot. Come on. We're almost there."

He slipped between two rhododendrons onto a well-defined path.

"I guess you've traveled this way in the past."

"Once or twice, compadre, once or twice."

At the end of the trail, Stogey peeped around the trunk of a huge cedar. Not to be left out, I climbed up and watched from above his head.

Over the next half hour, several people exited with the type of bags the store used for pastries. Each time Stogey said, "Too small, my boy, too small."

At length, a gray-haired man in walking shorts and an Atlanta Braves tee shirt emerged, carrying two flat white boxes.

"The mother lode, at last. Those cartons must hold three or four dozen doughnuts." Stogey glanced up at me. "Let's see where he goes."

The man stepped off the porch and down the walkway. He bypassed the parking lot and entered a broad trail leading to a nearby campground.

Stogey left his hiding place and skirted the clearing occupied by the general store, keeping out of view. "Let's go. He's played right into our hands. I know exactly what to do."

"What's that?"

"Follow along behind him. I'll go out onto the road where I can run and get ahead of him. Then I'll cut through the woods and head him off at the pass." He chuckled. "I've always wanted to say that." He raced toward the blacktop.

How could such a large animal move so fast? I snickered. Of course, he did have an abundance of the motivation he mentioned earlier.

Down the trail I trotted. Just as I caught sight of the tourist, Stogey burst out of the brush in front of him, raised up to his full height, and let out an ear-shattering growl.

The guy screamed, tossed the boxes thirty feet straight up, and passed me at about fifty miles per hour, twice the highest recorded speed for a human.

Stogey snatched both cartons out of the air before they hit the ground. He could do wonders when intent on a sugar fix. "Let's go. There's a pic-a-nic table right over here where we can enjoy our plunder."

He pushed through the brush for about forty yards to a lone table in a small clearing and popped open the top box. "Yum. Crullers. My favorite. Here, Zorro, have one."

"No thanks. A pear tree over there's full of fruit. That's my kind of feast." I scampered up a slight incline and climbed up into raccoon heaven. Hundreds of ripe pears surrounded me.

A while later, a scuffling sound grabbed my attention. I peered through the branches. "Stogey, run."

Mouth stuffed with the sweet pastries, he mumbled, "Don't bother me. I'm busy."

"But it's Ranger Jones, and he's got a tranquilizer gun."

He didn't move, which left it up to me.

I moved to a place where a limb overhung the trail and waited. When the ranger crept by, eyes focused on his target, I shouted, "Hey, ranger!"

He pivoted and looked up. I sprang from the tree, claws extended. When he raised his arms in front of his face, he lost his balance and fell backwards. The gun discharged into the air. He tumbled and came to rest face down. The tranquilizer dart descended and hit him right in the rump.

Wide-eyed, Stogey stared in my direction.

"It's okay now. You can take your time. He'll be out for hours." I returned to the tree and my own feast.

That afternoon, we lazed by a clear, clean trout stream. I smiled at my friend. "I love this place. It's so peaceful."

"Yeah, but it's been a long time since breakfast. I'm hungry. We need to search for something to eat."

"But, Stogey, the stream's full of fish."

"True. But fishing's hard work. And so-o-o-o boring. Besides, I prefer food with more pizzazz. Like pie. Or cake." He'd never realize that he expended far more effort to acquire sweets than it would take to catch his fill of trout.

"Oh, all right." I pushed to my feet. "Where to this time?"

He sniffed the air. "My keen sense of smell detects the aroma of apple pie." He turned and sniffed again. "This way." Off he lumbered in the direction of the nearest campground.

I caught him when he paused a short distance from the first campsite. Moments later, a lady emerged from a motor home carrying a pie. She strolled over and set it on a picnic table where a boy of about ten sat licking an all-day sucker. She placed her hands around her mouth as a makeshift megaphone. "George, Heather, time for dessert." With a smile, she headed back toward the camper.

Stogey nodded. "Easy pickings. Only a little kid between us and Nirvana. I'll do the scary act again. Works every time."

He stepped into the clearing and went into his routine. *Ro-o-oar!*

The kid's eyes widened and his jaw dropped. He threw the lollipop at Stogey. "Mom!" He sprinted toward the motor home.

The sucker hit Stogey above the left ear. Gooey candy stuck fast to his fur, and the stick protruded out to the side. What a hilarious sight. I choked back the urge to laugh. It might hurt my friend's feelings.

He tugged and tugged, but the contrary candy-on-a-stick refused to budge. He turned to me. "Zorro, buddy, come and get this thing off me."

He held out a paw and lifted me high. I scrambled onto his head. "I can loosen it, but I'll have to wash the stickiness off. It will take quite a while."

"Just do it."

I began to moisten the sticky area with saliva. After a few minutes, I rose up to catch my breath and glanced around. "Uh-oh. The ranger's truck is coming. Oh, no! Two more are behind him. He's called in reinforcements."

"Hop down, Zorro. Let's vamoose."

Across the campground he fled, into an open field used for softball games and Frisbee toss. He must not have noticed the college-age guy pushing a power mower. The worker wore shades and headphones, as if oblivious to his surroundings.

As Stogey crossed in front of the mower, he stumbled and tumbled headlong into a slight depression. The kid startled. The machine slipped from his grasp and zoomed forward, right over Stogey. For some reason, the kill switch hadn't stopped the engine...or the blade.

I ran to check on my friend. He lay where he fell, the fur on his left side shaved to the skin. He shook his head and sat up. "What happened?"

"A runaway lawn mower attacked you." I pointed to the affected area. "How do you like your new look?"

He stared at the denuded portion of his body, his mouth agape.

I bent over, picked up an object, and held it out. "At least it got rid of the lollipop."

A grin spread across his face. "Might as well make the best of the situation. Now, I'm Stogey the Bare."

Kid-Napped

A knock sounded at the door. Will pulled it open. Outside stood a middle-aged Irish goat with the tip of one long horn broken off. He held a tablet computer in one cloven hoof.

He scrutinized Will from head to toe. "William E. Goat?"

Will sighed. *Not again.* "It's spelled G-H-O-T-E and pronounced *Go-tay.*"

The visitor looked down his nose. "Very well. And your wife is Nancy *Go-tay?*"

"Yes, but everybody calls her Nan."

"I'm Declan O'Shaughnessy, a representative of the Planetary Revenue Service. Our records indicate your tax assessments for the last two years remain unpaid."

"Aren't you aware that as an operative for The Galactic Organization Against Trouble, all such collections from me are held in abeyance?"

The revenue agent touched his screen and scrolled down. "Of course. However, because more than two months have passed since your most recent GOAT mission, those obligations are now due."

He tapped his tablet again. "I forwarded an official notice to your communicator. You have ten days to file the required documents and render payment before interest and penalties accrue. Believe me, you don't want that. I'd advise you to pay up." He turned and strode down the sidewalk.

Nan came in from the kitchen. "Who was at the door?"

"Tax Collector. I'll be in the study paying our back taxes." Will stroked his beard. "Sometimes, I wish we goats hadn't emigrated from Earth and colonized this planet. Life was much simpler when we lived in the mountains and left the implications of civilization to the humans."

As Will clicked Send to complete payment, Commander Capra's face popped up on the screen of Will's communicator. "Ghote, report to headquarters, post haste. Sensors have detected an alien spacecraft headed in this direction ten thousand kilometers outside our atmosphere."

As Will stalked through the front door, Nan muted the television and looked up. "Back so soon, dear."

"Yeah, another false alarm from an overeager anti-invasion system operator. What a nincompoop. A drunk half-wit should have recognized the suspected invader as an interplanetary transport on its scheduled run. No need whatsoever to call in someone with my unique talents."

"You mean your ability to disappear and reappear at will?"

"Among others."

She giggled. "You sure make good use of that skill around here. Whenever it's time to take out the garbage, you vanish. At least, I'm never able to find you, but by the time I've washed my hooves after doing it myself, there you are. It's uncanny."

"Mere coincidence. I assure you." Not much chance she'd buy that one. He fought back a chuckle.

"Fifteen years of coincidences? I think not."

He shrugged. "It's a gift."

"Yeah, right." She snorted and rolled her eyes.

"Wives never give their husbands due respect." He stepped back and held himself erect. "I'll have you know, I'm a skilled investigator with commendations to prove it."

"Plaques on the wall or not, you don't seem to have the ability to locate the wastebasket. I find your abandoned newspapers all over the house."

He tapped one hoof. "I have more important matters on my mind than to concern myself with trivialities."

"Well, you'd consider those things less trivial if you found yourself up to your neck in trash."

He huffed and headed for the front of the house.

"Would you take today's paper and put it in the magazine rack?"

Ignore her. The best way to handle a nagging wife.

"I suppose selective deafness is another of your 'gifts.'"

He grinned but said nothing as he continued toward his study.

As Will pushed away from the dinner table two days later, the lights flashed, and loud beeps sounded from inside his study. A mechanical voice announced, "Red alert! Red alert!"

Will jumped to his feet and raced to answer the summons.

Commander Capra fidgeted as his stern face scowled at Will from the wall-sized screen. "What kept you?"

Should he defend himself? After all, he'd arrived mere seconds after the signal. No, better to soothe his superior's anxiety. "Sorry, sir. What's the emergency?"

"It's Admiral Buck. His son's missing."

"What happened? Did he wander off?"

Will's superior shook his head. "He's a toddler. I doubt he could walk far. Besides, his nanny just left him for a moment to take care of—ahem—a personal matter. When she returned, the window was open and he was gone."

"Could he have climbed out?"

"Unlikely. The window's too high off the ground. He'd have fallen and hurt himself."

Will nodded. "Suspicious circumstances, for sure."

"True. Although we have no specific evidence at this point, I suspect he might have been kidnapped. I need you here, Lieutenant. Now!"

"Yes, sir. I should arrive in about ten minutes." He shut down the computer, grabbed his portable communicator, and trotted into the kitchen. "Nan, it's an emergency! I'll see you when I see you." He gave her a quick kiss on the cheek and raced out the door.

Eight minutes later, Will parked his hovercraft in front of the admiral's residence, snatched his kit, and exited. Before he reached the porch, the door swung open and Commander Capra waved him inside.

"Good. You're here. This way to the kid's room." The commander led the way down the hall. "This situation calls for a thorough investigation. Don't overlook the minutest detail."

"Yes, sir. I'll examine everything with complete focus. You can count on me." Will set his kit on a bedside table. "Have you learned anything new?"

"No. Both parents were at work. The nanny already told us all she knows, and we've received no request for ransom."

"It's still early." Will held up his communicator. "I'd appreciate it if you'd keep me informed."

"I'll let you know if something breaks."

"Thank you, sir. With your permission, I'll begin my examination."

"Of course. I'll leave you to it. If you need anything, ask the sergeant outside the door."

"Will do." Where should he start? *Might as well check the likely means of egress first.* Will's gaze roamed over the window as he approached. Hmmm. Something didn't add up. What?

That's it. The size of the opening—too wide for a small child to have raised, yet too narrow for an adult to pass through. He lowered the sash a couple of inches. *Aha!* The window's cross pattern had concealed a tiny cut in the glass. No doubt used to unlock the window from outside. The odds of kidnapping had risen exponentially. But who had taken him? And why?

Will pulled out a magnifying glass and examined every millimeter of the windowpane, frame, and sill. No trace evidence around the hole, but he retrieved a dark gray hair caught under a sliver on the windowsill.

With practiced care, he extracted the specimen with forceps, and then studied it through the lens. He deposited the hair in a plastic bag, which he tucked into a pocket of the satchel where he kept his equipment. Then, he inspected the rest of the room inch by inch with the naked eye and the glass. Nothing relevant.

He strode to the doorway and peered around the jamb. "Sergeant, please ask Commander Capra to step in here."

A moment later, Will's superior arrived. "What is it, Ghote?"

Will led him to the window. "Look here."

"I see. No question that it's foul play, then?"

"No, sir, and there's more." He crossed the room and pulled out the evidence bag. "I found this hair caught on the sill."

"Left by an intruder?"

"No doubt. I figured you'd want to expedite the analysis. If you make the request yourself, it will receive higher priority."

"I'll take care of it right away. Do you have any ideas about who did this?"

"We'll need a scientific examination to confirm, but I expect the hair's canine. Canis lupus, to be precise."

"A wolf?" Capra touched the base of his neck. "How is this possible? We have the latest technology to detect invaders to our planet."

"I suspect they've developed a means whereby they can evade discovery."

The commander gasped. "By the hairs of my chin, this is far worse than I feared."

"We have our work cut out for us to catch these culprits. Wolves are sly. They won't give themselves away through carelessness."

"True. Still, I'm counting on you to get the job done, Lieutenant."

Will stood erect. "I'll do my utmost, sir. There's nothing more for me to do here. If you have no objection, I'll go to GOAT headquarters and review the surveillance records. Maybe I'll detect a minor abnormality that the operator failed to recognize. Perhaps careful study will provide a clue to when the invaders penetrated our defenses and where they went."

At nine o'clock the next morning, Will's communicator beeped. Commander Capra, his face grave. "We received a message from the kidnappers."

"A ransom demand?"

"Of a sort. If the admiral doesn't deliver all our secret defense plans, weapons systems included, by five p.m. tomorrow, they'll eat his son...and make him suffer in the process."

Will recoiled. "The beasts!"

"That's for sure. We must redouble our efforts to rescue the youngster."

"How do they want the plans delivered?"

"To an untraceable electronic address. No help there."

Will tilted his head to one side. "I assume you're attempting to trace the communication?"

"Yes, but they bounced the signal from planet to planet. It will take hours."

"When you identify the location, you'll find no indication of their presence."

"Most likely." Capra leaned closer to his camera. "Have you found anything on your end?"

"Nothing whatsoever. The invaders left behind no evidence of their arrival on the Planet Bovidae."

"You have to develop a new approach." The commander's brow furrowed. "We must stop them, or we'll all become prey for these savage beasts."

When the commander rang off, Will propped his face in his hooves. How could he locate the ingenious kidnappers? The situation seemed hopeless. *Wait a minute!* Voracious predators such as wolves had to eat often, and they couldn't have brought enough food with them to sustain them for long. If they had yielded to their hunger, he might trace them through reports of goats who'd vanished.

Where on this planet might they be? They'd choose a remote site, but not too far from the admiral's house in the capital. The invaders wouldn't want to remain exposed for a moment longer than necessary.

He pulled up a map of the region on his computer. Three likely possibilities presented themselves—a cave in the forest thirty kilometers east, a desert oasis fifty kilometers west, and a canyon in a mountainous area forty-five kilometers to the south. Now, for the missing goat reports.

Will accessed the law enforcement database and input his request. Seconds later, the report popped up. Twenty-two goats reported missing in the previous two days. Could he identify a pattern? Sixteen were last seen more than a hundred kilometers from any of the potential hideouts. One not far from the desert. Another near the mountains. The other four had disappeared within five kilometers of the forest cavern, although in different directions. Will scraped a hoof against the floor and snorted. The culprits had hidden their tracks, but not well enough.

Will crouched behind a boulder eighty meters from the cave in question. No sign of anyone yet. After a couple of hours, a large wolf in a gray uniform with a swastika on the sleeve exited the cave's mouth and strutted on his hind feet toward Will's location.

Another similarly clad canine goose-stepped forward, stopped, and held out one paw at sixty degrees. "*Sieg Heil, mein Major.*"

"What is it, Sergeant?"

"The scouts have captured another goat. Should arrive at any minute."

"Remind the men we're still on half-rations."

"Yes, sir." The noncom saluted again and rushed away.

Will stepped out. "I take it you're in charge of this enterprise."

Their leader pinned him with a disdainful stare. "And who might you be?"

"Lieutenant William Ghote of the Planetary Defense Forces."

"I'm Major Grayson Wulff, commander of the invasion force from the planet Canina." He glanced over his shoulder. "Hear that, guys?"

Five uniformed wolves streamed out from inside the cave.

"They send a single representative to intercept us and he's Billy Goat. Haw, Haw, Haw."

Will shot him his iciest glare. "*Nobody* calls me Billy."

"Ooh! He's getting his dander up. I'm afraid. Watch me tremble." He gave an exaggerated shake of one forepaw.

Will stood tall, arms crossed. "Enough chit-chat. Why are you here?"

"My pack came to scout this planet and establish an advance outpost preliminary to a full invasion. We mean to take over and make its inhabitants our slaves. At least, until we get hungry." After an evil laugh, he rubbed his stomach. His cohorts joined in the mirth.

"You might not find conquest as easy as you assume."

Wulff sneered. "What chance would mere goats have against the fiercest of canines?"

"Many of us, like myself, are mountain goats. We survived harsh weather conditions and escaped predators for millennia. Plus, some of us have powers you can't have anticipated."

"Special powers? Bah! Like what, eating rusty tin cans?"

At that moment, Will vanished.

The major did a full 360. "Where'd he go?"

"Right here." Will materialized behind him, and before the enemy commander could move, butted his backside. The major sprawled headlong into a mud puddle.

Will guffawed and pointed. "You should see yourself. Covered in muck. You're quite a sight."

"Let's see who laughs last."

When Wulff raised one paw, two of his pack grabbed Will from either side.

"Looks like we'll eat better tonight than we expected." The wolf leader poked Will's chest. "This old goat might be tough to chew, but we're equal to the challenge." He howled.

"Not so fast." Will eyed his chief adversary. "You don't really think I'd be foolish enough to come out here alone, did you? ... Now!"

Ten goats popped out from behind rocks and trees surrounding the wolfpack. Each held a taser in his hoof.

Wulff snorted. "You expect to defeat us with those? That's thirty-year-old technology."

"They may look the same, but we've made improvements. Mohair, zap the sergeant."

The goat nearest to Will pointed his device and pressed a button. Lightning flashed from taser to target.

The noncom dropped to the ground, then struggled to his feet. "Duh, what's going on? Where's my mama? I want my mama."

Wulff's eyes widened. "You've turned him into a blithering idiot."

"True, but it's not permanent. He'll be his old self in a day or two. Still, you might as well surrender."

"He's right, wolves. Paws up. The kid's in the cave—unharmed." The major hung his head. "How humiliating, a wolfpack captured by a bunch of goats."

"Mohair, take your squad and apprehend the scouts." Will pivoted and faced Wulff. "One thing I'd like to know. How did you reach our planet without detection?"

"We've developed a cloaking device. Makes our ships invisible even to the latest tracking equipment." The major gazed at Will. "What do you plan to do with us?"

"We'll send you packing. After you've told us all we want to know and we've reverse-engineered your spaceship's technology." Will grinned. "Oh, by the way, while you're our guests, you'll be on a vegetarian diet."

PART II
FRACTURED FAIRY TALES AND LEGENDS

From Little Red Riding Hood to Robin Hood to Santa Claus

Little Red Riding Hood Meets the Three Piggs

One fine spring morning, Little Red Riding Hood exited her family's cottage in the village, a cloth-covered basket on one arm.

"Red, tell Grandma I said, 'Hello.'"

"Okay, Mama."

Red smiled. She would have a lovely walk along the forest road. Her grandmother had moved back home a couple of days earlier, after she recovered from an illness that required constant care. Within a week or two, she would regain enough strength to cook for herself, but for now, Red brought Grandma her meals each day.

The damsel's departure did not go unnoticed. A wolf peeped out from behind a tree across the lane and salivated as he spied the delectable morsel.

Now, numerous misconceptions have arisen in telling and retelling Red's story. First, this wolf was no hairy canine, his fangs dripping with blood. A wolf only in a figurative sense, he was, in fact, a traveling salesman. In the worst tradition of traveling salesman stories of yesteryear, he had chosen his occupation less for lucrative sales than for the nubile farmers' daughters he might seduce.

Morcover, Red's appellation has misled numerous storytellers into thinking her a child. Our heroine was not a little girl in the ordinary understanding of the term, but merely diminutive. Although but four feet ten inches tall, she was a comely, well-proportioned lass of two and twenty, much pursued by unattached males in the vicinity, and not a few attached males, our villain included.

At first sight of Red, the wolf determined to have her. He stalked her through the woods but found no way to work his wiles while on the path. Any overtures would send her racing homeward and lead to pursuit by a horde of angry villagers. No problem in itself. He'd become expert at evasion, but he didn't relish such a chase without savoring the fruits beforehand.

The wolf's eyes lit up. *Aha, I'll rush to her grandmother's house. Once there, I'll figure something out.* How many dwellings might lie along this pathway? He'd find the right one with little difficulty.

Sure enough, the trail ended at a clearing in which sat a single cozy, vine-covered cottage. *Must be Grandma's house. I'll turn on the charm. She'll never know what hit her.* The wolf collected himself, smoothed his clothing, hand-combed his hair, and swaggered to the front door.

The door swung open before he knocked. Someone inside said, "Red, I've been waitin' for you...Oops! You're not Red. Who're you and whaddayuh want?"

An elderly woman stood in the doorway, her gray tresses pulled back into a bun. Bent over and supporting herself with a cane, such a weak, frail person would provide no challenge.

He pasted on his best 200-watt smile. "My name is Lobo, and this is your lucky day!"

"Whatcha talkin' about?"

"I can place in your home a beautiful set of Encyclopaedia Britannia at no cost to you. You'll be the envy of your neighbors."

His words came out rapid fire to give her no opportunity to interrupt. When he stopped to take a breath, Grandma crossed her arms. "Don't need no books. Cain't read. Ain't got no neighbors. D'yuh see any other houses 'round here? Nobody visits me 'ceptin' my granddaughter, and she cain't read neither."

She pushed with all her might against the door, but Lobo's strategically-placed foot forestalled the attempt. Plus, sales resistance fazed the master salesman not a whit. He had an answer ready for every objection.

Lobo pulled out his sample volume. "Just look how pretty they are. They'd brighten any home, and, if you'll permit me to say so, your cottage needs brightening."

Opening a brochure, he pointed to a sketch. "I'll also throw in this lovely imitation oak display case."

She turned from side to side. "Place *is* a mite drab. You'd better come in and tell me more."

Lobo hesitated not a moment. In a flash, he entered, overpowered Grandma, bound her, and threw her into the pantry. Without delay, he donned her nightgown, robe, and sleeping cap. While he adjusted the nighttime headwear, a knock sounded at the door.

"Grandma, are you okay?"

After a moment, the door cracked open. A head peeked in. "Grandma? There you are. I can hardly see you in the dim light."

Lobo's pulse raced. This winsome wench would provide a delightful interlude in an otherwise tedious week.

As Red swung the door wide, sunlight streamed into the room. Yet, Lobo remained in half-light. She stopped in the doorway. "Grandma, what big eyes you have."

"The better to feast them on you, my dear."

"Grandma, what big feet you have."

"The better to bring me close to you, my dear."

"Grandma, what big arms you have."

"The better to hold you, my dear."

"Grandma, what big lips you have."

"The better to kiss you, my dear."

The imposter lunged for Red, which brought him into full sunlight. She started, jumped back, and evaded his grasp.

"You-you're not Grandma!" She turned, raced out the door, and around the house.

Red might not be able to outrun the wolf, yet with her quick wit and nimble feet, she should manage to outmaneuver him. Avoiding the path to the village, she zigzagged through the timber.

She knew the forest well, but in her fright, lost her bearings. She stopped and listened. No sounds of pursuit. Now what ought she to do? She'd run in a straight line until she emerged from the woods. With luck, she would recognize her surroundings. Otherwise, she'd seek assistance.

After what seemed like hours, our heroine found herself in a lush, green meadow. Limbs heavy with fatigue, she struggled to set one foot in front of the other. At last, she spied some type of dwelling in the midst of the clearing.

Red fought her way through hip-deep grass. At length, she reached the structure, a tidy little place built of straw. If only someone inside could direct her toward her village.

She approached the door. Since it, too, was made of straw, she couldn't knock. Instead, she called out. "Hello, is anybody home?"

The door opened and revealed the householder, a young pig. Her hands flew to her chest, but within seconds, she regained her composure. Beggars couldn't be choosers. She would act as if it were of no consequence.

She launched into the speech she'd rehearsed over the last several hours. "Good afternoon, my name's Red."

"I'm Primero Pigg."

"I'm lost. I'd appreciate it if you can help me find my way."

"You look exhausted. Come in. Rest. I'll fetch you some water. Then we'll discuss how I can assist you."

Red entered the little house, which contained no furniture, but the straw-covered floor called her name. She lay down and fell asleep before he left the room. A shout roused her from her peaceful nap.

"Little pig, little pig, let me come in!"

As Red sat up, Primero thrust his front hooves onto his hips. "Not by the hair of my chinny-chin-chin."

He turned to her, now wide awake. "It's that blasted wolf, making a nuisance of himself again."

From outside came a loud growl. "Then I'll huff, and I'll puff, and I'll blow your house in!"

Red gulped. *This is a real wolf. Our lives are at stake. Not only my virtue.*

Her host grasped her hand. "Come on. He means it, and he can do it, too. Let's vamoose."

Primero parted the straw on the rear of the house and motioned her through ahead of him. Once outdoors, he whispered, "We must go to my brother's house, where we'll be safe."

They kept low, hidden by the grass, as they crept across the meadow to the timber. As they entered the edge of the wood, the roar of a rushing, mighty wind reached Red. She turned just as the straw house flew to pieces.

"I've got you now, little pig. I'll have roast pork for dinner!"

Primero took her hand. "We'd better make tracks before he discovers we've flown the coop."

He led her through the woodlands. They took care to make no sound, lest the wolf had followed.

As the sun set, they left the forest. Sand surrounded them. Both hills of sand and valleys of sand. He made a beeline for a house atop the highest sand hill. When they drew near, Red could make out a cleverly-designed dwelling fashioned from sticks of various shapes and sizes.

He shouted, "Segundo, are you home?"

The door sprang open. Another pig, similar to the first, but somewhat less plump, rushed out. "Primero, it's good to see you. What brings you to my humble abode?"

"It's that dratted wolf! He blew my house down! Again! We came here for shelter."

"We? Oh, who's this?"

"Meet Red. She got lost and came to me for help. The hairy, hungry beast showed up whilst she slept."

Segundo shook her hand. "I'm pleased to make your acquaintance, Miss. Sorry about the circumstances. You ought to be safe here tonight. Tomorrow, we'll help you on your way."

The three went inside the stick house, sat on stick chairs around a stick table, and partook of the meal Segundo provided. The food looked and smelled like nothing she had eaten before, but due to her fierce hunger, she dared not ask what it was. It filled her stomach, at least. While they ate, Primero recounted their encounter with the wolf. Afterward, she told both Piggs about her confrontation with a wolf of a different sort.

After dinner, they retired. A gracious host, Segundo offered her his bed of saplings padded with leaves, while the brothers bedded down on the floor. They awoke with a start at dawn, when someone pounded on the door.

"Little pig, little pig, let me come in!"

"Not again," groaned Primero.

Segundo yelled, "Not by the hair of my chinny-chin-chin!"

Their host turned to his guests. "Follow me. I have an escape route."

Through a concealed back door, he led them outside, down to the foot of the sandhill, and across a sand valley.

"Then I'll huff, and I'll puff, and I'll blow your house in!"

As they rounded a bend, the rush of a strong wind pummeled them, bringing with it numerous cracking sounds. Soon, wooden fragments flew past. Red and her companions hurried through the vale, and at last, reached the trees. A voice rang through the forest. "Where are you, little pigs? I mean to have you for dinner. You'll never escape."

Primero gazed at Segundo. "There's still one place where we can find shelter."

"You're right. He won't be happy to see us, but I doubt he'll turn us away with the wolf on our heels."

They traveled all day through woodlands and emerged at dusk into a world of stone. Neither grass nor other vegetation adorned the area, nothing but huge boulders. They climbed and climbed, reaching the pinnacle soon after dark. Before them stood a sturdy brick house. Primero gave a hesitant knock at the door.

A third pig, not unlike the others but lean and wiry, pulled open the door. With narrowed eyes, he crossed his arms. "You two, again. Didn't you learn your lesson the last time?"

"You won't let the wolf eat your brothers, will you?"

"I ought to, just to teach you to reject laziness." After a glance beyond his siblings, he frowned. "I see you're not alone."

He took a step toward Red. "I'm Tercero Pigg. Welcome."

"Everyone calls me Red."

"Young lady, how did you hook up with these two losers?"

She told him as he ushered them inside.

"An intriguing tale. You can all stay here tonight. You'll be quite safe. That windbag will never blow down my brick house. We'll sort everything out in the morning."

A shout woke them at dawn.

"Little pig, little pig, let me come in!"

"This has grown tiresome," grumbled Primero.

"Not by the hair of my chinny-chin-chin!" shouted Tercero.

The wolf huffed and puffed, and he puffed and huffed. But, try as he might, he couldn't blow the brick house down.

As the wolf was about to give up and slink off in disgrace, a man approached. With furrowed brow and tense muscles, the wolf faced him.

"Hello, I'm Lobo." The newcomer struggled to catch his breath. "We ought to join forces."

"B. B. Wolfe, here. Before you ask, B. B. stands for Big Bad. My parents had a warped sense of humor. Now, what's this about combining our efforts?"

"There's a young woman inside with three pigs, correct?"

"So?"

"She's so scrawny she'd provide little more than a nibble for you but a luscious treat for me. Let's work together to draw them out. You get those fat, juicy porkers, and I get the girl."

"It's a deal. What do you propose?"

By reading the encyclopedias he sold, Lobo had learned much, including how ancient warriors used catapults to breach fortified walls.

Near the forest's edge, the cohorts erected a huge catapult powerful enough to reach the brick stronghold. Stones were plentiful. The coconspirators loaded and launched a good-sized one, which landed fifty feet short of the house. A second struck seventy-five feet beyond it.

Although Red couldn't read, she was no fool. A stone would strike the house soon. Not even a brick structure could withstand that. "Those stones will crush this place. We need to escape. Now."

Tercero threw open a rear window. Red climbed through, followed by the Piggs. Tercero showed them a hidden route down through a cleft in the rock. As they reached ground level, a resounding crash resounded.

He wiped away a tear. "My beautiful home!"

Before they gained the shelter of the forest, a frantic voice rang out. "Look, they're getting away. After them."

They ran as far and as fast as they could, but, alas, the brothers were unaccustomed to such exertion and soon tired. When they stopped to rest, the sounds of pursuit drew nigh.

A tall, handsome man in rustic garments rushed into the clearing, a shotgun slung over one shoulder. His eyes lit up when his gaze landed on Red.

She eyed him. "Who are you?"

"Hunter Woodman. Do you need help?"

"Beyond doubt. I'm Red. These are the three Piggs. We're being chased by wolves, one with four legs and one with two."

Hunter nodded as if he grasped her meaning. "I'd be happy to assist you."

The pursuers burst into the meadow. Hunter aimed and fired. B. B. Wolfe bit the dust. Lobo turned tail and ran. Hunter discharged his second barrel, peppering Lobo's backside with buckshot. Lobo grabbed the burning body part and accelerated. He did not stop until he reached the king's prison, where he spent the remainder of his days employed as a guard. No women allowed.

The three Piggs reconciled and moved together to London, where they managed the city dump.

Hunter and Red fell in love. They married, and at last count, had six little Woodmen.

And they all lived happily ever after, including Grandma, who eloped to Monte Carlo with a handsome silver-haired peddler who happened by and rescued her from the pantry.

Previously published in
White County Creative Writers Anthology 2018

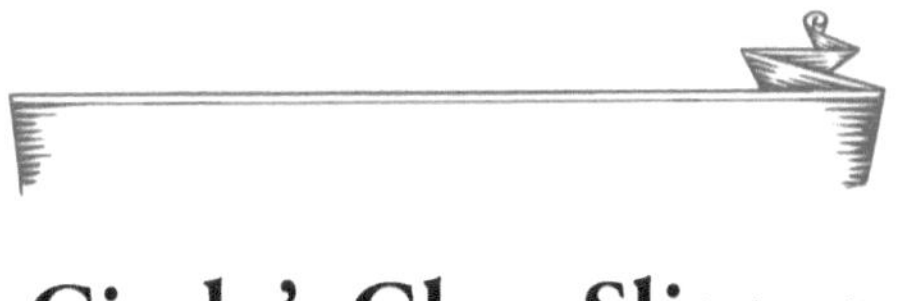

Cindy's Glass Slipper

I could dance all night. Cindy glanced up at the prince's handsome face. She had danced every dance with him since their eyes met from across the ballroom.

As the waltz ended, a clock started to chime. *Oh, no! Midnight.* She pushed her way out of his arms and dashed toward the door. She dared not let him catch sight of the real her. What utter humiliation she'd suffer.

"Wait, milady. I must see you again."

One shoe dropped off as she raced down the stairs outside the palace. No time to go back for it. She slipped off the other and held onto it as she sprinted around the corner to where her coach awaited. Before her eyes, the golden conveyance reverted to a pumpkin. The six white horses again became mice, and the liveried coachman a rat. Her beautiful, elegant pure white gown turned into dingy, filthy rags. No longer a glamorous woman of mystery, she had again become Cinderella, the household drudge. With shoulders slumped, she slinked away.

The next morning, while Cindy scrubbed the floor on her knees, her stepmother rushed into the drawing room and raced over to her two daughters who reclined on twin chaise longues. "Girls, I have exciting news. The prince fell in love with a young lady who dashed out of last night's ball at the stroke of midnight and left behind a glass slipper. He's searching the kingdom for the woman it fits. Make yourselves your most beautiful and don your finest gowns. You want to look your best when he stops here."

Late that afternoon, a footman announced the prince's arrival. Cindy scrambled away and hid in an alcove off the drawing room.

Moments later, a servant entered. "Madam, His Royal Highness, Crown Prince Rupert."

As Cindy peeped out after he passed by, Stepmother curtsied. "Welcome, Your Highness. We're honored by your presence. How might we serve you today?"

"I understand you have lovely maidens in your household."

She nodded. "Your Highness, may I present my daughters, Drucilla and Hildegard, the fairest lasses in the land."

"Ladies, I seek the damsel I wish to wed, the one whose dainty foot fits this glass slipper. Please, try it on."

Cindy retreated further into the alcove.

"Dash it!" Drucilla said, "It's much too small."

"I cannot even squeeze my foot into it," groaned Hildegard.

"Do you have other nubile women in the house?"

"None but my ragamuffin stepdaughter who did not attend the ball."

"Summon her at once."

"Right away, Your Highness...Cinderella," she screeched, "come here, this minute."

Cindy crept from her hiding place and shuffled into the drawing room on weak, shaky legs, her eyes downcast.

"His Highness wishes to speak to you."

"Yes, ma'am." Her chin trembled.

"Young lady, please take a seat." With a smile, he motioned toward a nearby chair.

After a poor attempt at a curtsey, Cindy sat on a nearby straight chair, without a word. The prince picked up her foot and slid the slipper onto it. Of course, it fit perfectly. He lifted her chin and gazed into her eyes. "It *is* you."

"Yes, Your Highness. I'm the one you danced with at the ball."

He turned to her stepmother. "Madam, I desire to wed this maiden. Do I have your consent?"

"Wouldn't you prefer one of my daughters? Either would make you a far more suitable bride than this...creature."

"No, I have made my choice."

"Then, I have no objection."

"Milady, please accompany me to the palace. My mother, the queen, will see you properly outfitted and prepare you for our wedding in a fortnight's time."

Cindy's heartbeat accelerated to a gallop, her hands tingled, and her grin threatened to split her cheeks. *Unbelievable!* Mere moments ago, she had been an abused outcast and now she would soon become a princess. She bowed. "Yes, Your Highness. I shall do as you ask."

He took her hand and assisted her to her feet. With a bow to her stepmother, he led her from the room. Once outside, a footman gave her a hand up into a fine carriage. A moment later, the prince, her future husband, sat beside her.

At his order, the coachman's whip snapped, and the conveyance lurched into motion.

She still could not believe her good fortune. The girl called Cinderella, in derision by her stepsisters, was on her way to the royal residence. There the queen would take her in hand and prepare her for marriage to the Crown Prince, the handsomest man in the Kingdom of Verdentia. What a tremendous blessing!

While they drove, the prince's countenance began to change, his once erect stature stooped. What was happening?

Cindy looked away toward the window. "Say, this is not the route to the palace. Where are we going?"

Her companion gave an evil laugh as the last vestiges of his handsome countenance melted away. His head grew larger with a heavy brow, hideous features, and a greenish complexion. "Why, to my lair, of course."

Oh, no! I've fallen into the hands of Daerg, the fearsome ogre of Verdentia. Dear God, what will become of me?

Cindy shuddered. "What do you plan to do with me?"

Daerg cackled. "I *will* wed you, as agreed."

"Nay, I consented to wed the prince, not...*you*."

"Although I looked like him at the time, it was I you promised to marry. And marry me, you shall. I'm the one who has you, and I intend to make you mine. You have no choice in the matter."

Her muscles tightened as her thoughts focused on the best way to escape. She would *never* submit to his demands, but her most effective action at present would be to act as if resigned to her fate. She stared out the window and forced her body to slump in her seat, hands clenched in her lap. Still, her mind remained alert, vigilant lest a chance to flee presented itself.

Daerg smirked, tossed his head back, and looked down his nose at her. "You would do well to make every effort to please me. Life will go better for you if you do. I determined to have the most beautiful maiden in the land for my bride, and I *always* get what I want. I'll be the envy of all my friends once they lay eyes on you."

He leaned back in the seat and crossed his arms, a self-satisfied smile on his face. "I devised the perfect plan to find The One and make her mine. First, I loosened a wheel on the prince's carriage and followed it. When it came off, I slipped into the wood nearby. While the prince waited for his men to make repairs, I imitated a small child calling for help and lured him into the forest. Then I overpowered him and left him bound in a hidden, secluded cave. After that, nothing remained but for me to transform myself into his likeness, don his clothing, and assume his identity. I traveled to the place where his now-repaired carriage had broken down and, in a perfect imitation of his voice, ordered the coachman to return to the palace in time for me to dress for the ball. Clever, wasn't it?"

He turned and stared at Cindy. "You see. You might as well give up any thought that you might outwit me. Not once has anybody bested me in a battle of wits."

He snickered. "I stripped the prince naked. If he should free himself, he'd find a journey home difficult since it would be unseemly for anyone to observe a royal in such a state of undress. Besides, without the trappings of his position, who would recognize him or believe his claims of royalty?"

Thoughts raced through Cindy's mind. What a horrible existence awaited her unless she managed to save herself. Somehow. But what would be her best strategy? Oh, yes, she would feign acquiescence. Remain listless as she complied with his every demand. Perhaps he would grow overconfident and relax his vigilance, which would provide her the opening she sought.

A week later, Cindy donned a luxurious white wedding gown, assisted by Vorga, her ogress watchdog. "You will give Daerg great pleasure this day. He has summoned friends from afar to witness his marriage. They'll turn green with envy." She chuckled at her joke. Many ogres were already green.

Daerg hadn't allowed her a moment alone. A guard armed with sword and spear stood sentinel outside the door, and her ever-present "companion" never left her side.

Time had grown short. If something didn't happen soon, she'd have to do something desperate or find herself wedded to the gruesome beast.

"Fiddlesticks!" Vorga shook her oversized head. "This veil has a rip in it. I'll have to take it to the seamstress for repair." She stormed from the room.

Cindy's heart rate galloped. She must escape now, or she might never have another opportunity, but how, with the door guarded?

She ran to the open window. The ground loomed at least ten yards below. If she jumped, the fall might kill her. Yet, she'd prefer death to a lifetime as the ogre's wife. She climbed onto the sill and dropped.

A second later, she struck the earth with force. *Ouch! That hurt.* Cindy pushed to her feet, brushed herself off, and raced into the nearby forest, ignoring the pain in her knees and ankles. No telling how much of a head start she'd have.

Sounds of pursuit soon reached her. She increased the speed of her flight. As she glanced over her shoulder, she ran into something solid and bounced to the ground.

When she raised her eyes, a man in rough clothing leaned over her. Were her eyes deceiving her? "Prince Rupert?"

"Yes, it is I. How did you recognize me? We've never met." He extended a hand. "Let me help you up."

Once on her feet, she said, "The ogre impersonated you at the ball, an exact double. I'm happy to find you in good health. Daerg said he bound you and left you in a secluded cave. I feared for your safety."

"After I freed myself from the bonds, I 'borrowed' this attire off a clothesline behind an isolated cabin. I'll compensate the owner when I return to the palace. After I dressed, I chanced upon a wayside tavern. Inside, everyone discussed the mysterious maiden who danced for hours with the prince. A footman for a local noble witnessed her flight at midnight. He regaled the crowd with stories of how the prince searched the kingdom for her and then vanished."

Cindy sighed. "Of course, it was the ogre masquerading as you. He located me. Told me he wanted to marry me and take me to the palace to prepare for the wedding. Instead, he took me to his lair—a castle deep in the forest rather than the cave-like hideaway I'd anticipated."

"I figured as much. Hence, I came to search for you. Thank the Lord I found you." He reached for her hand. "Hark, your pursuers approach. Come, let us flee."

After they'd run as fast as they could through the trees and brush for more than an hour, he grabbed her and yanked her back.

She gazed down into a yawning abyss. "What is this?"

"It's a sinkhole." The prince cocked an ear. "From the reduced noise level behind us, I suspect most of our pursuers have given up the chase."

Cindy shook her head. "Not Daerg. He'll never relent. He's determined to have me as his bride."

"True." He pointed at the chasm. "But this may provide our salvation."

"What do you mean?"

"Hurry. Let's cover it with brush and grass."

After a flurry of frenzied activity, he said, "This will do. Now, stand on the far side of the trap. Bend over with your hands on your knees, and pant as if too exhausted to go on. With luck, the ogre will be so thrilled to have found you that he won't take time to examine the ground before he rushes toward you. Meanwhile, I'll hide nearby."

Within minutes, Daerg rushed into the clearing. He stopped and thrust his fists onto his hips. "Aha, my pretty. You should have known you could never escape me. I *will* have you for my bride, this very day."

He strode forward, gaze fixed on Cindy. When he stepped on the brush, it gave way. His eyes widened as he dropped into the abyss.

The prince popped out from behind a tree. "That ought to take care of matters. Daerg will never again terrorize Verdentia."

"Now what? We're still lost in the forest."

"Not so, my dear. I recognize this place. I visited here often as a child." He pointed. "Just over yon hill lies the castle of my uncle, the Duke of Namora. He will provide us with transportation to the palace."

"The palace? Me?"

"Of course. Even in the filthy, torn gown, you're the most beautiful damsel I have ever seen. Your hair's like spun gold. I fell half in love with you from the stories I heard about the ball. Since the moment I met you, I've wished to marry you...if you'll have me."

Heat radiated through her chest as her face turned upward toward him. "You sought me and saved me. I'd be honored to become your bride."

He extended his elbow. "Shall we go, my dear?"

She placed her hand on his forearm. "Let's."

Cindy stepped to the door of the palace chapel as the orchestra played the introduction of The Wedding March. At the altar stood Rupert, her groom, resplendent in a dress uniform. She took the arm of the Prime Minister who escorted her down the aisle and handed her off to her prince. Together, they faced the bishop. A servant girl adjusted and straightened the train of her magnificent white gown, far lovelier than the one the ogre provided.

"Dearly beloved, we are gathered here to join this man and this woman in holy matrimony..."

"...I now pronounce you man and wife. You may kiss the bride."

Rupert turned, took her in his arms, drew her close, and lowered his lips to hers. Her pulse raced as she clung to him and poured all her love into her response.

Too soon, he pulled away, although he held on to her hand. "Later, my love," he whispered, "when we're alone, I won't have to hold back and can give full expression to my passion for you."

A grin tugged at her cheeks, which grew warm.

The bishop cleared his throat. "I now present to you Prince Rupert and Princess Lucinda."

Heat radiated throughout her body, and her heart drummed in her chest. No more a household drudge. No more filthy rags. Cinderella, no longer, she would make the most of her new life, a life far beyond her wildest dreams. The life of a princess, a wife, and one day, a mother. What more could a girl ask?

Allie's Lamp

Allie grunted as she turned over another shovelful of dirt. The sun beat down. Must have been ninety-five in the shade. Why had she gotten the brilliant idea to plant roses in her backyard, today of all days? Beautiful, of course, but what an exhausting project. As the garden center instructed, she'd dug a trench three feet deep and replaced the clay with a mixture of topsoil and organic material.

With a sigh, she stopped, wiped her brow, and rubbed her aching back as she surveyed her work. Deep and wide enough. A foot longer and she'd have room for the bushes she'd bought. Oh, well, she'd gone this far. Might as well finish the job.

Twenty minutes later, she sank the spade into the soil one last time.

Clunk!

What in the world? With the shovel, she scooped away the dirt she'd disturbed. A rounded shape lay partially exposed. She knocked off enough soil from around it to curl her fingers underneath and lift it out. What could it be?

Still in the trench, she tapped the object with her hand and shook off the loosened clay. *Aha!* A lamp similar to the one in the movie *Aladdin*. If it was that old, it must be valuable. Perhaps, priceless.

She clambered out of the hole, carried her find into the kitchen, and rinsed it in the sink. Sure enough, it *was* a lamp. Bronze, but tarnished as if long lost. How much would a museum pay for this?

She grabbed a cloth and buffed it with vigor. A puff of smoke rose out of her unique find. When the smoke cleared, a man dressed in colorful garb out of a production of the Arabian Nights, complete with white turban, stood before her.

"Who summoned me?"

Mouth agape, Allie stepped back. "Um...I guess *I* did."

"Why, you're only a slip of a girl."

She crossed her arms. "I'll have you know I'm twenty-four."

He smirked. "Ooh, practically in your dotage. Who, pray tell, are you?"

"Allie Dean. I—"

"Allie Dean and her magic lamp?" He cackled and slapped his knee. "You've got to be kidding me?"

"Nope. That's my name. And who might you be?"

He rolled his eyes. "I'm the genie who lives in the lamp. I've enjoyed a peaceful life for the last thousand years and now this." He exhaled with a dramatic sigh. "What do you want?"

Her breath caught in her chest. "Uh...I'm not sure."

The genie thrust his hands onto his hips. "Come on. Out with it. I have better things to do than stand here and jaw with you. What's your wish?"

"You mean you'll grant my request?" Her limbs tingled. "Anything I want?"

"That's how it works." He sighed.

"Okay. I'll have a steak dinner with all the trimmings."

When he snapped his fingers, a sizzling T-bone, baked potato, and salad materialized on a spotless tablecloth, complete with fine china and silverware.

In a flash, Allie took a seat at the table and sliced into the meat. She turned to face the genie. "This steak's well done. I prefer mine medium-rare."

"Tough. You asked for steak. You got steak. You didn't specify. I'm outta here. Don't bother me. Fatima's waiting, and she's the epitome of feminine allure."

Rats! Just Allie's luck to get a genie with attitude.

"I don't understand, Paul." A tear trickled down Allie's cheek. "We've dated for two years. I thought you brought me to Arturo's to propose, not to dump me."

"I'm sorry. I didn't want to hurt you, but there's someone else."

She swallowed. Hard. "Why, Paul?"

As he shrugged, his gaze followed a shapely girl who wandered past. "Well, for one thing, Brianna's a beauty. And you're...you." His eyes bugged out as if to emphasize the point. "Come on. I'll take you home."

Heat flushed through her body. "Forget it! I'm not ready to leave. When I am, I'll take a taxi. Just go." *Jerk!*

When the door closed behind him, she jumped up, darted to the restroom, and hid in a stall, where she could cry in private.

Forty minutes later, Allie paid the taxi driver, trudged up the walkway, and entered her house. What was wrong with her? Why didn't anyone love her? She was neither hideous nor insufferable. So why did she seem destined to live a life of loneliness?

Her gaze landed on the lamp, which sat on an end table. Maybe she had a way to get a man, after all. She took a seat on one end of the couch, picked up the ancient relic, and rubbed its bronze belly.

The genie materialized amidst a puff of smoke. He wore nothing but a towel wrapped around his waist and held a long-handled brush in one hand. Through clenched teeth, he hissed, "Not you again. What's so important that you have to interrupt my bath?"

With a frown, she tilted her head downward. "My boyfriend left me for someone prettier. I want you to make me beautiful."

"Very well. You asked for it." He shoved both hands toward her. "Abracadabra!"

In an instant, she turned into a blue and white porcelain vessel. "Argh! Not what I meant, and you know it."

"You're a Ming vase. What could be lovelier?"

"Enough of that."

His eyes narrowed. "Oh, all right. Alla-kazaam!"

Allie glanced downward. She'd become herself again. "I meant a beautiful woman. The kind men find desirable."

"I can do it, but are you sure you want men to pursue you for your looks alone?" His brows rose.

Old Grouch Pants might have an attitude but, for once, he made sense. "I guess not." She swallowed hard. "I'll stay as I am."

"Time I returned to my bath. If you're *quite* finished?"

She waved a hand. "Go ahead. If I'm doomed to live forever alone, I might as well make the best of it."

The genie vanished into the lamp.

She stared at her hands. Hollowness filled her chest. "Sometimes, I wish I could get away from it all. Find a place to live in peace. Where other people wouldn't complicate my life."

A too-familiar voice rang out from inside the lamp. "I heard that."

An instant later, Allie found herself surrounded by trees draped with spider webs. Little light penetrated the thick canopy of leaves. The wind whined like a dog with a wounded paw.

She shivered. "This place is creepy. Where are we?"

"A place where dreams come true. Ignore the forest's foreboding fringe. It discourages potential invaders." Beside her, the genie waved a hand. "Follow me. If I give you your heart's desire, maybe you'll leave me in peace."

He strode off at a frantic pace down a path through a gap between the trees.

"But I..." Oh, well. She had no choice but to follow.

After a while, she stopped, panting. "How much farther is it?"

"Impatient much?" He cocked his head, then shook it. "It's not too far. I take it you need a rest?"

"Yes, please. I'm not used to treks through the forest. And besides—"

"Very well. I'll check in with Fatima while you take five." With that, he faded away.

She dropped to the ground and leaned back against a tree trunk. Her eyes drifted shut...

Allie's eyes popped open. Had a voice sounded somewhere behind her? She twisted and peered around the tree.

Whoa! Unbelievable. Three pigs sat at a picnic table outside a small, tidy brick house with bowls before each of them. The largest sipped from a spoon. "You know, this wolf stew isn't half bad." All three snickered.

"Ready to go?"

Allie's gaze snapped to the front, where Old Grouch Pants stood tapping his foot.

She said, "I'm beyond ready to go—"

He dashed away.

"—home." With her lips pinched together, she struggled to her feet and scampered after him. Maybe he'd listen, sometime.

After a while, they entered a clearing. To one side sat a stone tower, perhaps thirty feet tall. A handsome young man dressed in elaborate medieval attire stood looking upward. "Rapunzel, Rapunzel, let down your hair."

A braided golden rope dropped from an open window high in the tower.

As Allie passed, the man reached toward the rope. What kind of place was this? And why did those sable locks, chiseled features, and square jaw look familiar?

She hurried along the path. Wouldn't want to fall too far behind Old Grouch Pants.

Before long, seven tiny men in pointy shoes, each with a different tool over his shoulder, whistled a tune as they marched past. A beautiful raven-haired girl scurried after them.

This was a most unusual forest. Still, she had no desire to be here. The place they were headed to had better be good, or the world might soon be short one genie.

As they reached another clearing, a little girl with honey-blonde braids burst out of a stone cottage and raced away. Seconds later, a bear in a pink dress with a matching purse and pumps stepped into the doorway and shouted, "Sorry, sweetie. We didn't mean to scare you. You're welcome here anytime."

Allie shook her head. *This gets weirder and weirder the farther we go. It's time to call a halt to this expedition and go home.*

The genie stopped. "We're here. Right in the center of the forest." He snapped his fingers.

The trees receded. In the midst of the cleared area, a house materialized out of nothing, from the ground up.

Once completed, the dwelling resembled Allie's, minus the peeling paint and saggy roof. Around the house lay an impeccable garden filled with roses and all manner of other flowers in beds separated by gravel paths lined by neatly trimmed hedges. In the center of the garden in front of the house was a koi pond filled with colorful fish.

The genie beamed. "Well, what do you think?"

"It's gorgeous. A perfect retreat." She cleared her throat. "But not what I want."

"You—"

She held up a hand. "Let me finish. I'd had a bad day and was venting. I didn't really want to isolate myself from other people," — she waved a hand around her — "like this. Please, take me home."

He muttered something unintelligible under his breath, but she could make out a single word—*ungrateful.* He sighed. "All right, if you insist."

"**K**nock, knock."

Allie glanced over her shoulder toward her office doorway. "Come in, Eugene. I need help."

As the company's tech guru approached, he pushed his thick-lensed, horn-rimmed glasses up his nose. "What's wrong?"

She smiled at the oft-repeated gesture and tapped the monitor. "This computer froze when I attempted to post a job description. I don't know if it's my workstation or the system."

"Did you reboot?"

"I tried...but nothing happened." She stood and moved to one side.

He took her chair. "Let me see." His fingers flew over the keyboard. "Uh-oh."

"What is it?"

"Your motherboard's fried."

"I can't work without my computer. What'll I do?"

"I'll bring you a loaner and transfer the data off your hard drive. Should have you up and running within the hour. Ought to have you a new one in a week or two."

"Eugene, you're a miracle worker. What would we do without you?" She bent over and hugged him.

His face turned red. "Um...be back in a few with the loaner." He rushed away.

She'd embarrassed him. Had it been the praise or the impulsive hug? *Oh, well.* She surveyed the room. Stacks of folders occupied every inch of surface area. Clearing away the clutter would keep her busy while Eugene worked his magic. Too bad she didn't have the lamp here at the office. Her genie could organize everything with a snap of his fingers.

As the last of the dishwater gurgled down the drain, Allie gazed out the kitchen window. A delightful, sunny day. Saturday morning with nothing on her schedule. How marvelous to have a whole day to relax and catch up on household chores. But on such a nice day, why stay cooped up inside? She draped the dishtowel over the faucet and made a beeline for the back door.

Once outside, the flowerbed caught her eye. After six weeks, the rosebushes she'd set out had yet to thrive. Several plants had turned brown. Others looked wilted, and the handful of blooms drooped. She'd done everything the guy at the nursery told her to do. Yet she'd gotten *this*. Not much of a return for all her hard work. What could she do to produce healthy, beautiful roses? Nothing...unless...*the genie.*

She dashed inside, returned with the lamp, and rubbed with gusto.

Soon, her genie popped out, arms crossed, and with a scowl on his face. "What now? A thirty-room mansion? A new Rolls Royce?"

"Nothing so grand. I just want my roses vigorous and lovely."

He yawned. "You've interrupted my *siesta* for this?" With a shake of his head, he waved one hand toward the rosebushes and disappeared in a puff of smoke.

Within seconds, huge full blooms in vivid red, yellow, and pink filled lush, green bushes.

Magnificent. With a wide grin, Allie pulled a lawn chair over to where she could sit, stare, and admire the beauty. Her genie had come through for once. Since he'd handled this task well, even though her summons irritated him, perhaps he would do the same with more crucial requests.

A llie glanced over her shoulder. "Eugene, I can't believe you got me this lightning-fast computer. It's incredible. Thank you."

"Well, I did have to talk fast to get Mr. Thompson to okay the additional expense, but you deserve the best." Pink filled his cheeks. "This model ought to meet all your needs for several years and help you accomplish more in less time."

She pivoted in her chair and faced him. "You make me feel special."

"You *are* special." His flushed cheeks turned crimson, and he scurried out the door as if his tail were on fire.

Allie's gaze remained fixed on the doorway. What a nice guy, if somewhat timid.

She shook her head. Time to get back to work. *Now, where did I put the Reynolds report?* Oh, yeah. Left-hand bottom drawer.

When she'd pulled it open, she picked up the desired folder. Underneath lay the headshot of Paul she'd shoved in there to get it out of sight. She grabbed the photo and tossed it into the trashcan, frame and all. Too bad her ex wasn't more like Eugene. If so, she might not have to spend her life alone.

A llie's phone rang. "Hi, Mom."

"Happy birthday, sweetheart."

She dropped her dishtowel and took a seat at the kitchen table. "Thanks, Mom. How's Alaska?"

"You wouldn't believe how gorgeous. But you sound down."

Her shoulders drooped. "Maybe a little."

"You said you didn't mind if your father and I took this cruise over your birthday."

"I'll be fine." She sighed. "Enjoy your trip."

"Oh, we will. But we want you to have a good day."

She forced herself to smile. "I will. I promise."

"I've got to go. It's time to explore a glacier."

"Bye, Mom. Tell Dad I said 'Hi.'"

"I will. Goodbye, dear."

Now, how could Allie keep her promise? Twenty-five years old today with no husband, no kids, and no prospects. Her stomach clenched.

Allie's gaze meandered around the room until it settled on the lamp. Aha! Maybe she'd have a chance for happiness, after all. She grabbed her bronze prize, stepped out onto the deck, and rubbed with vigor.

The genie swooped out and stood before her, lips puckered and arms circled as if wrapped around someone. Eyes narrowed, he looked left and right, then thrust his hands onto his hips. "What is it this time?"

"Sorry to drag you away from Fatima, but—"

"Fatima is so last month. It's Layla now, but she's already grown stale." He eyed Allie from head to toe. "Say, you don't look half bad. Ever visited Baghdad? How about a ride on a magic carpet?"

"Not exactly my cup of tea, although I *am* lonely. I'm interested in a permanent relationship. Someone who'll love me forever."

"What a disappointment you are. I might have shown you the delights of the Casbah and revealed the mysteries of the East. But, alas, you desire nothing more than a drab, humdrum existence. What a pity. I refuse to be a party to the waste of such delightful assets." He snapped his fingers and vanished.

A screen door banged from the direction of the vacant house next door. A handsome hunk of a man with chiseled features and dark, wavy hair strode toward her. "Hello, neighbor."

"Hi."

Who was this fellow who approached with such self-assurance?

"You don't recognize me, do you?"

She cocked her head. Where had she seen a similar square jaw and jet-black hair? "You look familiar, and I ought to recognize the voice, but I can't place you?"

"I'm Eugene, your tech support guy."

Her head jerked back. "Um...I'd never have known you. What happened to your glasses?" No wonder the fine-looking fellow at the tower in the forest had caught her attention. He looked just like Eugene, minus the specs.

"Lasik surgery." He turned his head from side to side. "What do you think?"

"You look...great." *Like a different person.* "But what brings you here?"

"This morning, I closed on the house next door." He turned and extended his hand in that direction. "We're neighbors."

Allie's heart drummed in her chest. Her gaze fell on the lamp. With a nice guy, gorgeous now, right next door—one who'd discovered a newfound confidence—who needed help from a genie? Especially such an ill-tempered one? She'd replant that relic by the rosebushes.

With a wide smile, she stepped closer. "Welcome to the neighborhood."

Days of Yore

"You've got to be kidding!" Doubled over in laughter, Will set down his glass on the university cafeteria table and forced himself to sit up straight. "You actually believe someone can pass through a portal to another time? Besides, you need to begin researching your dissertation. Why waste time on such rot?"

Bradley matched Will's intense gaze. "I've done considerable reading on the subject. Respected scholars have studied time travel."

"Ridiculous." Will scowled. "All speculation. There's no hard evidence."

"Still, I find the ancient texts persuasive."

"Pure fiction."

A gleam filled Bradley's eyes. "I'm nearly certain I've found one."

"What? A passageway into another time?" Will rolled his eyes.

"Correct. Not far from here."

Will jumped up and rounded the table. "This I've gotta see."

That afternoon, Will dogged his gullible friend's steps down the barely-discernible trail. "Are we almost there?"

Bradley pointed ahead. "Beyond the rise."

Moments later, he stopped beside a hole about four feet across. "This is it."

With a smirk, Will shook his head. "You brought me way out here to see a sinkhole?"

"Not at all. I dropped a stone in. It has no bottom."

"From that, you've concluded it's a portal into another time?"

Bradley nodded. "Yup."

"You need a keeper. I'll bet you chose a pebble so small you couldn't hear it hit. Here, I'll show you."

Will picked up a softball-sized rock and strode to the edge. Loose gravel rolled under his feet, the ground gave way, and he tumbled into darkness.

S omething pricked Will's neck.

"Who be ye?"

He opened his eyes and did a double-take. He lay propped against a tree. A man in a forest green tunic leaned over him. Was this a weird dream?

"I asked 'Who be ye?'"

Again, a sharp object jabbed him. "Ouch! What do you think you're doing?" *Good grief! That's a sword. What have I gotten myself into?*

A second voice boomed. "I wager he's a spy."

The man in green said, "You'd best answer, ere I skewer your gizzard."

"W-will. Will Lett." He rubbed his right cheek. "Some call me Scar. And you are?"

"Dobbin of Rockley." He stepped back and faced left. "Meet my friend, John. Often dubbed, 'Dribble John.'"

No wonder. Drool oozed down the man's chin.

"John's not the brightest torch in the castle, but a fair hand in a tussle. Behold the size of him." Dobbin swept his hand around. "And these are my band of Dairymen."

"Dairymen?"

"Aye. A vicious plague struck our cattle. Wiped out the living of all on my estate. We retreated into Durwood forest to survive. Enough about me. Whence come ye?"

With a scratch of his head, Will stared at his inquisitor. "First, where am I?"

"Know ye not that ye be in the East Midlands?"

"Of England?"

"Aye. Where else?"

Will perused the odd garments worn by his inquisitor's companions. "What year?"

"The Year of Our Lord 1191." Dobbin's brows lowered.

Breathless, Will opened and closed his mouth several times. "You won't believe this. I'm from the future. The year 2025."

"Nay, I cannot give credence to your claim."

"I'm from North America, a land beyond the sea. I'm uncertain how I got here, but I must have fallen through a portal from my time to yours."

Dobbin gaped, wide-eyed.

Someone shouted, "Hark! Riders approach."

"Prince Don's minions, no doubt. Disperse."

The Dairymen disappeared into the brush. Seconds later, a hand yanked Will behind the tree. When he recovered his composure, he gazed up at his savior—John. Who else?

As the clip-clop of hooves faded, one man reappeared. "You were correct. The Sheriff of Rottenham. With his swordsmen."

Dobbin glanced at Will. "Prince Don's chief henchman in this region."

Will chuckled. "*Rottenham?*"

"Raises swine. You can smell his estate for miles. Come on, Will, join us."

"I guess I have little choice. What now?"

"We forage for food. Our families depend on us. No easy task since the cattle died. We suspect the sheriff infected them. The price of pork has trebled."

"Is there sufficient game?"

"At first." Dobbin sighed. "Now, we must range far to find as much as a rabbit."

"Can't you raise enough vegetables to keep yourselves fed?"

"Aye, but Prince John's taxes take the bulk of them."

"How, then, do you survive?"

"From time to time, a merchant or noble donates his purse to the cause. At the point of a sword. Also, one of the sheriff's pigs vanishes, now and again. Let us hasten to Rottenham Castle. It's time for him to make another contribution."

Dobbin parted the brush at the forest's edge two hundred yards from the moat.

The aroma of cooked meat reached Will's nostrils as he squeezed in next to his new friend. "What's happening?"

"A feast."

Will peered through the gap. Dozens of well-dressed men roamed the expansive meadow, tankards in hand. Pigs impaled on spits roasted over open fires.

Will glanced at Dobbin. "Won't it be difficult to liberate a pig with all these people present?"

"Nay, when everybody gets drunk, 'twill be easy pickings."

Will scanned the crowd until his eyes beheld a vision. Golden hair framed an oval face and cascaded to a slender waist. The luxurious crimson gown did little to hide the damsel's ample charms. He gasped. "Who's that?"

"You must have spied the fair Marianne, Rottenham's ward."

"She's extraordinary."

"And has the good sense to despise Rottenham. Sometimes she rides in the forest. Would you like to meet her?"

Two days later, everyone scattered as hoofbeats approached.

"Dobbin, are you here?"

At the melodious feminine voice, Will followed Dobbin and the Dairymen out of the hidden camp.

The sheriff's young ward sat sidesaddle, lovelier still with windblown hair. Will's heart tugged.

Dobbin bowed. "Welcome to our humble abode, Fair Marianne."

"Dobbin, cease your jest. Help me dismount."

He stepped nearer and offered his hand. She took it and slid to the ground. Eyebrows raised, she looked Will up and down, from buzz cut to Reeboks. She turned to Dobbin. "Who's your friend?"

He made a sweeping gesture. "My new comrade, Will Lett. Will, may I present Lady Marianne d'Aurlene."

Will gave a poor imitation of a courtly bow. "Pleased to meet you, milady."

She curtsied in return. "And I you. Dobbin, you've rubbed off on him."

Will grinned. "It's only your due, milady."

Her indigo eyes captured his. "I implore you to cease this 'milady' foolishness at once. Call me Marianne."

"Very well, *Marianne*." His face heated.

She faced Dobbin. "I've raided Rottenham's larder. The poke's tied to my saddle. Have someone fetch it, would you please?"

After a brief visit, she stood. "I must bid you adieu. Rottenham will miss me soon. Will, would you kindly escort me to my horse?"

"My pleasure, mi—Marianne."

When they reached her noble steed, the beautiful maiden turned to Will. "'Twas a delight to meet thee."

"Meeting *you* was beyond wonderful, lovely Marianne." He took her hand, bowed, and kissed it.

"You're unlike anyone I've ever known."

"You have no idea."

She raised on tiptoe and bussed him on one cheek. "Would you assist me, kind sir?"

With a strength he knew not he possessed, for she was a buxom lass, Will lifted her onto her mount. "Farewell, fairest of the fair."

She laughed. "Good bye. I hope we shall meet again. Soon."

"As do I." *More than you know.*

The next day, a horse approached the hideout at the gallop. "Dobbin! Dobbin! Help!"

He rushed into the clearing. "What is it, Marianne?"

"A lad from the village stole a piglet. Rottenham and his men are en route to burn the settlement. You have to do something."

"If I show myself, he'll forget his plans and pursue me." Dobbin helped her dismount. "I must borrow your horse to arrive in time. Will, stay here and care for Marianne. Men, follow in haste."

Seconds later, Will and Marianne alone remained in the glade.

"Tell me, Will, from whence do you come, and why do you differ so from other fellows?"

"I come from across the sea and a time eight hundred years in the future."

Her mouth fell open. "I perceived your odd speech and clothing, but never anticipated such an answer. How came you to this place?"

"The details of my arrival don't matter. Only that I am here. Tell me about yourself."

Marianne explained at length how Rottenham assumed guardianship upon her father's death five years earlier and his increasing insistence that she marry him. Not only did he want to possess her but also to annex her family's lands. "I must escape his control. Can you help me?"

"I'm not sure how, but I shall."

"Thank thee, Will." She kissed his cheek. Again.

"You'd best stop that, or I'll be tempted to kiss *you*. And not on the cheek."

A flush spread over her visage. "Would it be so bad?"

"That's the problem. It wouldn't be bad at all."

Her blush deepened.

Pounding hooves announced Dobbin's return. He dismounted and handed the reins to Marianne. "We've distracted them for the moment. I left my men behind, so I could give back your horse. If you hurry, you'll reach the castle before Rottenham."

Will boosted her into the saddle, and she galloped away. Far too soon.

Later, the Dairymen filtered into the glade.

Dobbin hopped up on a stump. "Men, Rottenham's getting out of hand. We must deal with him once and for all. What say ye?"

One Dairyman spoke up. "He's hidden his ill-gotten gains. If we find his treasure, we can feed the entire shire, and he couldn't afford his soldiers, which would render him powerless."

"Any ideas on how to locate it?"

Will stepped forward. "Pressure him so he has to tap his reserves. He'll have to visit his hideaway. Have someone to watch and follow him wherever he goes."

"Excellent. We shall launch a series of raids to take what coin he has at hand. We begin at dawn. Will, you're the best person to spy on the blackguard."

A week later, the sheriff appeared behind the castle and vanished into the forest. He must have a secret exit. Will made haste to keep him in sight.

After several minutes, Will peeked around a tree. Before him yawned a cave with a stone door open beside it. Rottenham exited carrying a heavy leather bag and swung the door shut. He scanned his surroundings and hurried down the path.

Will emerged from hiding and examined the door. Covered with brush, it blended into the hillside. He pulled a patch of greenery aside, revealing an odd-shaped hole, like the Greek letter delta inside an omicron. A unique keyhole, perhaps.

When he reached camp, he told Dobbin what he'd found. "But we can't access it without the key."

"I expect Marianne soon. Mayhap, she can help."

After she arrived midafternoon, Will explained the situation. "Do you know where he keeps the key?"

"I've never seen it, but he keeps an object on a chain around his neck and never takes it off."

Will nodded. "That must be it."

Dobbin stood, fists clenched. "We have to obtain that key."

Marianne said, "Rottenham hosts an archery tournament on the morrow. Everyone on the estate will be there. Dobbin, why not attend in disguise?"

"Might work. Will, you shall accompany me, but you'll need a priest's cassock to hide your peculiar garments."

The next afternoon, Dobbin entered the competition in the guise of a stooped old man. As he readied his final shot, Marianne dropped her kerchief. Rottenham bent to retrieve it. The chain slipped free and dangled from his neck. Dobbin shifted his aim and released the arrow, which severed the chain. The key fell to the ground.

Will rushed forward, struck the back of Rottenham's neck with a karate chop, leaned over, and grabbed the key. The sheriff staggered and collapsed.

Will clutched Marianne's hand and raced toward the cave where Dribble John and several Dairymen awaited. Will inserted the key into the hole. The door sprang open a couple of inches. John pulled it wide and led the men inside.

By the time Dobbin arrived, they had removed the gold and loaded it onto borrowed donkeys.

"Away, men. Our comrades can delay Rottenham only so long." Dobbin trailed behind them at a run.

Will turned to Marianne, whose hand he still held. "We did it."

She smiled at him, eyes alight.

The sheriff and his henchmen burst into the meadow and surrounded the two of them.

Will whispered, "Into the cave. It's our one hope."

She followed without hesitation. As they passed through the entrance, a crossbow bolt nicked his ear.

Deeper into the cave's dimness they ran, the clatter of their pursuers growing louder. Then everything went black.

Will opened his eyes. Trees towered above him. To the right rose a cliff. *Donnegan Park. It must all have been a dream.*

"Will, are you awake?"

"Marianne!" As she bent over him, he touched her face. "You're real."

"Of course."

"And beautiful." He slid his hand behind her neck and pulled her down until their lips met. When she returned his kiss, warmth spread to his toes.

"You saved me, as you promised."

His chest tightened. "Was that a kiss of gratitude?"

She shook her head. "Far more."

"Me, too, I love you."

"And I you. But where are we?"

"Dear Marianne. We're in *my* time now—together—and I have so much to show you."

Santa's Licky, Sticky Situation
Or Lucky Saves Christmas

Nick gulped the last of his milk and set the glass on the table beside the empty plate, which had held a half-dozen heavenly snickerdoodles. So sweet and tasty. Yum!

A burp slipped out as he rubbed his rounded belly. For the past six days, he'd eaten everything in sight, yet remained ravenous. *Blast that confounded doctor for prescribing Prednisone for my most recent asthma flareup.* Never again would Nick let the elves talk him into acting as referee for an outdoor hockey tournament a week prior to Christmas. He'd already put on eight pounds and wouldn't be surprised if he gained another five before he completed tonight's mission.

Well, time to go to work. He still had much to accomplish this night. He stepped into the fireplace, laid a finger beside his nose, and drifted up the chimney to the roof, where he tossed his sack into the sleigh and climbed in. "Dasher, Dancer, lead on to our next destination."

At house after house, he repeated the same procedure—drop down the chimney, leave the requisite gifts, and return to the sleigh. But on this Christmas Eve, he didn't just sample the milk and cookies at each stop. Instead, he gobbled down every bite in a vain attempt to quench his insatiable, gnawing hunger.

Yet, when he arrived at the Copeland residence in a small Arkansas community, everything changed. As Nick hopped off the sleigh, his knees buckled. Why? He bounced on his toes. Was he heavier than before? Perhaps he'd overdone it with the last snack. He shouldn't have emptied the plate, but oatmeal raisin cookies were his favorites.

Oh, well. Time to get back on task. He filled his sack with the gifts selected for the three children who lived there. Next, he climbed into the chimney and began his descent, as usual. About a foot from the bottom, he came to a sudden stop.

He kicked his feet, which swung freely. They must be dangling in the fireplace.

Although he wriggled and squirmed, he failed to move a millimeter. He tugged and pulled on the sides of the chimney, then pushed and shoved against it, but remained stuck fast.

Confound it! I should have remembered this chimney tapers toward the bottom...or resisted all those milk and cookies regardless of my hunger pangs.

What a disaster! How would he complete his rounds?

After an eternity passed, which was probably no more than five minutes in reality, a dog barked nearby. *Uh-oh!* This could present a problem. Sure enough, something tugged at the seat of Nick's trousers. Again and again.

"Watch out! You may bite more than — Ouch! You got me that time."

Another tug. *Ri-i-i-p!* There went another new outfit. *I hate when that happens.*

A child's voice rang out. "Hey, Lucky, you woke me up. What were you barking at? Say...what's this in the chimney?" Light footsteps drew nearer. "Those shiny black boots. The red suit. It's Santa!"

"It's me all right, young man. I'm stuck. Can you help get me out of here?"

"Sure. Lucky, grab his pants again."

Between the dog's continuous tugs and the boy's yanks, first on one leg and then the other, Nick inched downward. At last, he plopped into the fireplace. Ashes flew into the air. He sneezed. His sack fell after him and conked him on the head.

When the room stopped spinning, his eyes focused on Joey Copeland, the eight-year-old boy who lived in the house. Beside him sat a half-grown Great Pyrenees puppy, who must have weighed in at no less than eighty pounds.

Nick staggered to his feet and attempted to brush the worst of the ash and soot off his clothes. "Thanks, Joey. I don't know what I'd have done without your help." He smiled at the dog. "And Lucky's. Although my trousers are a trifle drafty."

"What happened?"

Nick rubbed his protruding belly. "Too much milk and cookies."

"I can see that. You look even fatter than usual." The youngster clapped his hand over his mouth. "Sorry. Mom says I have diarrhea of the mouth, that I have zero control over what comes out."

"Ho, ho, ho. It's okay, son, you didn't hurt my feelings, but your mother's right. You might offend others if you spurt out such things without thinking." Nick removed a half-dozen packages from his sack and filled the three stockings.

"Say, Santa, how will you slide down all the other chimneys and not get stuck again?"

Nick stroked his beard. "That presents a real problem, doesn't it?"

The boy nodded. "Sure does. A sticky one."

"Besides, even for the houses with chimneys large enough to accommodate a supersized Santa, it wouldn't do for me to risk having a child spy and catch me with my Fruit of the Looms exposed like this, now would it?" Nick turned his backside toward Joey.

The youngster snickered. "I guess not."

"I still have from here to California, plus Alaska and Hawaii, to cover. There'll be millions of disappointed boys and girls if I fail to complete my rounds." He couldn't bear to think of their sad faces if they jumped out of bed on Christmas morning and found no presents in their stockings or under the tree. "But I have a potential solution."

"What's that?"

"I'd like for you and Lucky to come with me."

The boy bounced up and down as a broad grin spread across his face. "Do you mean it, Santa?"

"Sure do. You can go down the chimney and put the toys in each stocking. Take your furry friend along to carry the sack for you. I'll have you back before your parents wake up in the morning. What do you think?"

Joey patted the dog's head. "Come on, Lucky. Let's go!"

The massive canine leaped forward and raised up on his hind legs, his forepaws on Nick's chest.

"Whoa!" Nick toppled over backward.

The pup ran over to him and licked all over his face.

"Ho, ho, ho." He scrambled to his feet, wiping off the wetness. "Looks like Lucky's ready and raring to go."

Joey cackled. "I guess so."

Nick looked the boy over from head to foot. "Since your pajamas have feet in them, that will work, but you'd better grab a coat, hat, and mittens. It's winter, and we'll have to move fast in an open sleigh."

He raced from the room and returned, seconds later, with one arm in a heavy overcoat.

Nick eyed the fireplace. "I think we ought to skip the chimney. Let's use the door."

"Good idea." Joey chuckled as he zipped up and donned a sock toboggan. "*Woof!*"

"I think Lucky agrees. Come on. Times a-wastin'."

Once outside the house, Nick took hold of Joey's gloved hand and placed a finger beside his nose. As one, the three floated to the rooftop, where they climbed into the sleigh. "Onward, trusty reindeer, we have far to go yet tonight."

The sleigh accelerated more slowly than usual and gave a slight dip as it left the roof. Dasher turned toward Nick, wrinkled his snout, and rolled his eyes.

Nick grinned. *I think he's trying to tell me something.*

PART III — GHOSTS MAGIC AND OTHER
SUPERNATURAL PHENOMENA

No scarier than Casper

Misfit

"**P**ie-erce!" The gruff, unearthly voice broke the silence.

Not again. Pierce gulped, or came as close as possible, given his current circumstances. Why couldn't he keep Augustus off his back? No matter how hard he tried, Pierce always got crossways with his supervisor. And when Augustus was unhappy, he never shouted. He shrieked.

Pierce trudged over to where Augustus stood, arms crossed, perpetual scowl in place. Of course, *nobody* pleased the old grouch, but he held a particular animus for Pierce. Why couldn't The Big Guy have given him a different mentor?

"You incompetent boob. You've failed again. I sent you and Creepy to haunt the Huntington mansion, but no-o-o. You fell asleep. You'll never make the grade. When the headmistress learns about this, they'll hear her howl all the way to Cucamonga."

"S-sorry, b-boss. I was exhausted." He attempted to stifle a yawn...to no avail.

"You'd better shape up, or I'll have you banished to Outer Darkness. You wouldn't want that."

Pierce shivered. He sure wouldn't. His head spun at the thought.

Augustus thrust his fists onto his hips. "Do you remember your assigned task for tonight?"

"Y-yes, sir."

Augustus leaned forward, inches from Pierce's face. "Don't mess this one up. Do you understand?"

"Yes, sir. I won't let you down this time. I promise."

Pierce surveyed his surroundings. Ah, this wasn't so bad. Nothing like the dark, dank Huntington place. Although The Bard Theatre had remained closed for decades, the glow of gaslights and the fire from the opening scene of Macbe—the Scottish play—still cast an aura of flickering light all around. This, he could handle. If only his assignment for tomorrow, long-abandoned Saint Agnes Hospital, was more like this.

He strolled down the aisle and leaped onto the stage. With a flourish, he twirled to face the non-existent audience. "Friends, Romans, countrymen, lend me your ears." His voice resounded through the empty theater.

Applause sounded from the center of the front row. Seconds later, Rosalie revealed herself. "Not bad, Pierce. Did you work as an actor before you crossed over?"

"Hardly. I wanted to be a comedian, but could never break into the business. I worked as a shipping clerk in a warehouse." A misfit all his life, and after, he hung his head. "What did you do?"

"I was a dancer. Made the chorus in a couple of Off-Broadway shows but earned my living as a waitress."

A disembodied voice rang out from the balcony. "Hey, you two, cut it out. We're supposed to act scary. Not reminisce about what never happened."

Pierce shrugged. "I guess Wormy Will's right. We'd better hop to it. If Augustus catches us, he'll have us drawn and quartered."

"How can you draw and quarter a ghost?"

"I'm not sure, but Augustus will find a way. Here goes nothing. *Woooooo.*"

Rosalie laughed. "You're about as scary as a newborn puppy."

"Too true. That's why I'm in remedial training." He winced. "I'm afraid it won't take."

"You'll figure it out. Try a screech instead. Like opening the gates of Hades. *Scree-ee-ee-eech!*"

Pierce sighed. He'd never pull this off, either. Didn't have the voice for it. Or the heart. Would he ever get the hang of this?

Pierce awoke to chains clanking in the hallway of the long-vacant hotel. What a blessing that his mentor had been a galley slave centuries ago. He couldn't sneak up on anyone.

He sat up in bed.

Augustus stuck his head through the door. Literally. A guy never got any privacy when his associates could pass through solid objects.

"Say, what's going on here?" Augustus surveyed the room but stopped when his gaze landed on Pierce. "Just as I thought. Asleep again instead of following orders."

Pierce vaulted out of bed onto the floor. "Sorry, boss."

"You addlebrained dolt! You're a disgrace to the profession." He glanced to his left. "What's this? You sleep with a night light? Aw, so cute, a little bunny. Now, ain't that sweet? What's the problem, goofball? Afraid of the dark?" Augustus rolled his eyes, or he would have if he had eyes.

Pierce trembled and turned white as a sheet, which didn't take much for him. Now Old Sourpuss would tell everyone Pierce's secret. A ghost afraid of the dark—he'd never live down the humiliation. No matter that he'd spent two days trapped under a table in a pitch-black cellar after a tornado at age four. Nobody would care.

"That's it, isn't it? No wonder The Big Guy sent you for remedial scare training. Not that I think, for a moment, it'll work. Wait 'til I tell the gang. They'll think it's a scream." He motioned towards the door. "You mosey down to the hospital right now. And for this trick, I'm assigning you to the mental ward. Ha-ha-ha."

Oh, no! Anything but that. Those poltergeists were insane. Hundreds of patients had died in there, locked in cells reminiscent of Pierce's cellar. Not to mention the brutal treatments. Spirits of many of those dreadful victims still hung around. Crazy in life, crazy in death. Those guys would frighten even the most accomplished ghosts. Pierce trembled all over.

It took seconds for him to fly the eight miles to the derelict medical facility. He floated toward the psych ward, which once occupied a separate building on the grounds apart from the hospital proper. No doubt, so the screams and wails wouldn't disturb the regular patients. After all these years, the sounds remained audible, but more macabre.

He hesitated outside the door, unable to cross the threshold. What a failure. A ghost himself, he knew spirits had no actual power to hurt anybody. Besides, with him already dead, what could anyone do to injure him? Yet, he couldn't force himself to enter the frightful place.

"Are you sure you want to do this?"

Pierce whirled around. Who was that? Someone must be coming. He rendered himself invisible.

Three teenage boys crept toward where Pierce waited. One snarled. "What's the matter, Spencer? You chicken?" The ringleader, no doubt.

"No, but I don't want to get in trouble."

The leader stopped, hands on hips. "Not happening. Nobody ever comes here anymore. But they say the joint is haunted. It'll be fun to explore and find out if we can scare up a ghost."

Pierce materialized in front of them, hands raised as if to grab them. *"Wooooooo."*

Spencer jumped back. "Y-you're a r-real g-ghost?"

"In the flesh. Well, not quite—but here I am, anyway. Disembodied spirit at your service."

The ringleader reached out and tried to touch Pierce, but his hand passed right through.

"See, I told you. I'm an honest-to-goodness spook. Believe me. You *really* don't want to go inside."

The third boy spoke up for the first time. "But you're not scary."

"No, but I'm not your ordinary ghost. Those guys in there—they go way beyond the norm. They terrify *me*."

"You're kidding. I'm not scared of nuthin'." The leader again. Mister Macho.

"Okay, go ahead, but don't say I didn't warn you."

"Come on, fellows. Let's go in." Macho Dude grabbed Spencer's arm.

"Not me." Spencer shook off the fellow's hand. "I'll stay right here."

The third teen said, "Me, too."

"What a couple of chickens." With a sneer, Mister Macho pulled the door wide and stepped inside.

The other two teens glanced at each other and shrugged.

Pierce lowered his voice. "Don't worry, guys. He won't want to tell anybody anything about tonight. Just wait about two seconds."

The door burst open, and their oh-so-brave leader, paler than Pierce, streaked past screaming.

"I tried to warn him, but he wouldn't listen. You boys might want to go on home now."

"Thanks, Mister Ghost."

Pierce smiled. He'd done a good deed.

"Pierce! You imbecile. You're supposed to be inside helping to frighten those kids. Not out here warning them."

Pierce jumped. How did Augustus do it? Somehow, he had avoided the telltale chain rattle and caught Pierce unawares. "What are you doing here?"

"My job. Unlike some haunts I could name." Old Grouch Puss pointed. "Get yourself in there, this minute. Or else."

Pierce flew through the closed door into utter darkness.

"And don't come out before morning."

Screams and other eerie sounds bombarded him from all sides, but Pierce could see nothing at all. His heart would have raced and pounded if he still had one. Dizziness crept over him. Though not visible, the walls seemed to close in.

Someone screamed. Another bawled with wracking sobs.

"*Eeyie.*"

"O-o-o-o-h!"

"Ha, ha, ha, ha, ha."

Pierce wrapped his arms tight around his body and huddled in one corner. He remained there until dawn, shuddering all over. It was the worst night of his death.

At first light, Pierce made his escape.

As soon as he passed outside, Augustus appeared. "You surprised me. Actually stayed in the booby hatch all night. Perhaps I was wrong about you. As a reward, I have a plum mission for you tonight. The McNulty house downtown. Old Mickey McNulty has haunted the place ever since his wife poisoned him over a hundred years ago. He can teach you a lot about the business. But don't forget to show up before midnight."

At ten o'clock that night, Pierce landed on the porch of the vacant mansion. No lights showed inside, but a streetlight located right outside the front window would illuminate the rooms somewhat. This might not be so bad.

"Hey, Mistah. Are you a ghost?"

Pierce spun around. A little girl of about four gazed up at him, eyes wide.

"I am." Why was she out by herself at this hour?

"I thought ghosts were supposed to be scawwy."

Pierce bent down to her level. "You don't think I'm scary? Boo."

The youngster giggled. "I like you. You're funny." She trotted back to the sidewalk as a woman approached. Her mother?

Good thing Augustus hadn't heard that exchange.

"Pie-erce!"

Uh-oh. No such luck. He'd recognize you-know-who's shriek anywhere. He was in for it now.

With a scowl fiercer than usual, his trainer whooshed up to him, so angry his ectoplasm had turned crimson. "You're an embarrassment. A ghost should scare people, not make them laugh. You can't even frighten a child."

"But it's a lot more fun. Did you hear the one about the ghost who was so scary he scared himself to death?"

"You call that a joke? You'd never make it as a comic. Better keep your night job. With that in mind, I'd urge you to become serious about your lessons, or else." He gave Pierce a fierce glare. "In fact, after this latest escapade, you'd best report to the headmistress at noon tomorrow. She'll set you straight. Now, go in there and let McNulty mentor you."

Pierce passed through a wall into the primary reading room of the abandoned Osbourne Library, which housed the remedial training school. While he hovered outside the office door, he slumped. This was it, the equivalent of a kindergartner sent to the office of a principal rumored to have an electric paddle. Decades' worth of spiderwebs swathing the empty shelves that lined the walls added to his sense of impending doom.

The headmistress ruled her domain like a marine drill instructor. To make matters worse, her parents in life had named her Fanny, a prescient decision since, even as an apparition, her rear end measured two axe handles wide. So, whenever Pierce caught a glimpse of her, he struggled to keep from laughing his head off, metaphorically speaking.

"Pierce!"

He turned and faced the spookretary who'd materialized next to him.

"Don't dilly-dally. Get in there."

"Yes, ma'am." He swept through the closed door.

Fanny sat behind an enormous mahogany desk. A blessing. With her lower half hidden, maybe he would make it through this session with a straight face.

She scowled. "Augustus tells me you're not making progress. Recommends that I put you on the list for Outer Darkness." She held up a folder. "Based on these reports, his assessment seems apt. What do you have to say for yourself?"

He stiffened his non-existent spine. "No excuse, ma'am. I'm a flop at scariness."

"I find that hard to believe. We just haven't found your niche. I don't want to give up on you yet. I'll allow you one more chance."

"Thank you, Fanny."

"Well, if you promise to listen to Augustus and follow his directions for the next week, I'll try to come up with a permanent assignment to match your temperament."

"I'll give it my best shot."

"Very well." She motioned toward the door. "You may go."

For seven days, Pierce gritted his teeth, figuratively, and endured assignments to a deserted army barracks, a disused railroad depot, and three nights at a Revolutionary War graveyard.

As he prepared to leave the next evening, Fanny's spookretary stopped him at the door. "The headmistress wants to see you. Right away."

Pierce quivered like a sheet on a clothesline in March. This might mean oblivion. No sense in putting it off. He glided down the hall and into the headmistress's office.

"Sit." She waved toward a chair. "I have something to discuss with you."

No scowl this time. Perhaps she'd give him good news. He took the indicated seat.

"I believe I've found an excellent place for you. A perfect fit."

"Thank you. I'll try to meet your expectations."

"You will. Don't worry. Report at once to 4377 Spruce Street."

"Yes, ma'am. Right away, ma'am."

Pierce flew through the door and continued on to the address she'd given him, a warehouse-like building in a blighted area near the waterfront. Might as well get this over with. He passed through the brick wall into the interior.

A specter with horn-rimmed spectacles and a pork pie hat zoomed up and met him. "You must be Pierce. We've been waiting for you."

Pierce scanned his surroundings. Blackened brick walls lined the room. Dozens of spooks of all shapes and sizes sat in rows in front of a lighted stage. What in the world? "I don't understand."

Mr. Specs pulled him toward the wings. "I'm Soapy Sells. I run this theater. Welcome to Blythe Spirits' Komedy Klub. A fire back in '59 killed two hundred performers, staff, and spectators. We've haunted the joint ever since."

"Why am *I* here?"

"Didn't they tell you? You're our headliner. The warm-up act finished seconds ago. You're on."

Pierce floated onstage and assumed a position behind the microphone. Bright lights flooded him, yet the audience remained visible, more or less. This was his kind of place. *Thank you, Fanny.*

He launched into his best routine. "A funny thing happened on the way to the theater tonight. A ghost glided up to me and said, 'I haven't had a bite in a week.' I looked him over and said, 'You think you're skinny now? Wait until you've been dead for a hundred years.'"

Laughter broke out and resounded off the walls.

Pierce beamed. "Have you heard the one about..."

Immaterial Witness

Nathan sighed as he unlocked and opened his front door. What a long day. Longer week. With his assistant on maternity leave, he'd worked sixty hours.

He closed the door behind him, trudged into his study, and laid an armful of folders on his desk. So much for the prospect of a restful weekend. As he turned, a sharp blow to his chest knocked him backward a couple of inches. How was it possible with no one else in the room?

Nathan struggled to draw a breath. A wet, warm sensation spread across his upper body. He glanced downward. A crimson stain covered his shirt. His vision blurred. His legs buckled. Everything went black…

Nathan studied his surroundings. He stood in the foyer outside his study. Who were all these people running around in his house? And where did the little round hole in the window come from?

A pudgy man, silver at the temples, in a rumpled gray pinstripe with a gold badge at his waist, walked in without knocking. He passed Nathan as if he weren't there and joined the others in the study. "What've we got?"

A woman in a white lab coat faced the newcomer. "Gunshot wound in the center of the chest. No other apparent injuries. Probable cause of death, although I won't know for certain until the autopsy."

Incredible! Someone shot in *his* house. Murdered! The killer must have fired through the window. The victim lay out of sight behind all those people.

The detective bent down. "Time of death?"

"Liver temp suggests three to five hours ago."

"Thanks, Doc."

"You're welcome, Lieutenant. Can we have the body now?"

"Sure."

Two young men separated from the others, hauled a gurney over, and lifted the deceased onto it. As one pulled a blanket over the corpse, the group parted, which gave Nathan a clear view of the room.

Oh, no! It's me! I'm dead. Murdered.

If he was no longer alive, then he was a ghost. No wonder the lieutenant acted as if he'd failed to see him. But why was he still here? He must not be able to rest, to move on, while his murder remained unsolved. So, he would have to make sure that changed. As a microbiologist, he had learned to follow clues and solve difficult mysteries, such as the causes of various diseases. Why couldn't he do the same with his own death?

As a disembodied spirit, he could gain access to information the detectives didn't possess. He also had the ability to go places unobserved, but he'd have to find a way to communicate anything he discovered to the authorities.

A uniformed officer opened the door and entered the police station. Nathan darted in at the cop's heels. Once inside, he stopped. *What a doofus.* Why bother to wait around and sneak in behind someone? Walls presented no barrier to a ghost. He extended his hand. Sure enough, it passed right through the glass door.

Now to locate the lieutenant in charge of the case. On the wall hung a directory. An entry about halfway down indicated that the detective division occupied the third floor. He walked through the closed door and floated up the stairs. On the far side of the room, the officer he sought sat at a scarred metal desk. The nameplate read, "Lt. Hanrahan." A man and a woman, also in plain clothes, perched on chairs across from him.

"Okay, Marchetti, where do we stand?"

"Dr. Nathan Rafferty, Professor of Microbiology at the university. Specialized in research. No known enemies." He handed the lieutenant a folder. "The autopsy report just came in. No surprises. Cause of death...a single gunshot wound to the heart. Penetrated the right ventricle. Victim died between ten p.m. and two a.m."

Hanrahan nodded. "Fits with information from our neighborhood canvas. Several witnesses reported hearing a car backfire around midnight."

Nathan shook his head. Closer to a quarter after. He'd left the office about five minutes before twelve.

Hanrahan glanced toward the attractive thirty-something female. "What have you got, Lopez?"

"Ballistics called a while ago. Bullet was a nine-millimeter. Fired from a Beretta. In good enough shape to identify the gun...if we find it."

"How are we doing on that score?"

"Uniforms searched trashcans and storm drains within a half-mile radius. Nothing."

"The murderer must've taken it with him." The lieutenant's gaze ping-ponged between his two subordinates. "Have you identified anyone with a motive?"

Marchetti spoke up. "Not yet, but we're still questioning people at his office. His ex-wife's out of town, so we haven't interviewed her. Should return tomorrow."

"Does anybody profit by his death?"

"No family. Parents deceased. His only brother died in Iraq. No kids. He left his estate to the university where he worked, earmarked for research. Not such a large sum that someone would be likely to kill him to fund a project."

Hanrahan frowned. "Which means we're nowhere."

"Correct."

"Okay, keep me posted."

The police had made little progress. It was up to Nathan to discover who hated, or feared, him enough to commit murder.

Nathan strolled along the lake. Whenever he wanted to mull things over, he came here. Something about the water, the sky, and the trees calmed him. Helped clear his mind and organize his thoughts. Perhaps it would still work after his death. Of course, he'd never faced a situation like this one.

The officers were correct. Nobody would benefit from his demise. Yet, he must have done something to make an enemy want him dead, but what? He had always tried to treat people right. Even though he and Michelle couldn't live together, they'd managed an amicable divorce. Still met for dinner on occasion. She'd have no reason to harm him.

What about professional rivalries? Dr. Horvath at the state university *had* wanted the research grant—bad—and resented its being awarded to a small private institution. Although single-minded and ambitious, he wouldn't stoop to violence. Professor Fabian would take over leadership of the project now, but she preferred to remain in the background. She would never kill for the opportunity. Nobody else in academia stood to gain by his death.

Who did that leave?

He walked on for twenty minutes, but no other potential suspect materialized. So, he must have done something to offend somebody or seen something he shouldn't. What if he retraced his steps over the last week? He might recall something to give him an idea.

Over the next three days, Nathan worked through every place he'd visited and all his actions over the previous six. He had gone to work, eaten at different restaurants, sometimes with friends, and passed time at home. All routine. Nothing stood out.

He sighed. All this time wasted with nothing to show for it. Maybe he should drop this project as futile. No! He refused to let his murderer get away with the crime. He'd review his activities for all of the preceding week as planned, then reassess.

Time to consider the seventh day before his death. He had spent Saturday around the house. Caught up on his housework and mowed the lawn. Watched a football game on TV. Nothing unusual, except the Razorbacks beat LSU, for a change, on a last-minute touchdown.

Hold on! A high school buddy he hadn't seen in years had dropped by and taken Nathan to dinner at a new Italian place downtown. He'd go there tonight and attempt to recreate what happened. Perhaps he witnessed something at the restaurant he shouldn't have—such as a man he recognized cheating on his wife—but failed to take note of it.

An attractive lady in front of him downed the final bite of her lasagna.

As best he could tell, he'd spotted no one he knew on his previous visit to Giuseppe's. Though he and Patrick lingered after they finished their meals and drank a gallon of sweet tea while they filled each other in on their years apart, nothing out of the ordinary occurred. Until they prepared to leave...

Patrick tossed a couple of twenties on the table as he stood. "It's late. I'd better drop you off and hurry back to Mom's. She'll wonder what kept me."

"You know, I feel restless. I think I'll walk home..."

At last, a glimmer of hope. Maybe something had happened on his homeward stroll. He needed to retrace his steps. Nathan's insides fluttered as he drifted toward the exit.

Outside, he hung a left and followed the most direct route. His gaze darted from side to side as he walked. Had anything occurred that slipped his mind?

After a half-mile, he turned right into a neighborhood of older apartment buildings reconditioned as part of an urban renewal project. Fifty yards ahead, a couple of streetlights were out.

When he entered the dark section, an image of two shadowy figures standing on the stoop of a building across the street in the middle of the block flashed into his memory. The door had opened and briefly illuminated the men as one passed a thick white envelope to the other.

Nathan tingled all over. Although he'd paid no attention at the time, this must be it. Who were they? He replayed the scene in his head again and again. Both seemed familiar. Oh, well, it would come to him. He continued his journey.

As he drew nearer to his place, Nathan's route took him through a neighborhood business district. A streetlight overhead cast light upon a newspaper vending machine in front of a drugstore. A headline screamed: "Cappucci murder trial begins tomorrow." Nathan stopped and studied the paper. Two photos graced the front page—District Attorney Scott Morris and the accused, Jonathan Cappucci.

One of the men outside the building that night had been Scott Morris. The other, though older, looked much like the picture of Jonathan Cappucci. Nathan would bet anything the second man was Jonathan's father, Niccolò Cappucci, head of a local crime family.

Now he was getting somewhere. One of those two must be responsible for Nathan's murder. But which one?

What should Nathan do with this information? The DA had met with a gangster and apparently received a bribe, but Nathan couldn't prove it. Nor point out his killer. This situation called for reason.

If the Cappuccis were behind his murder, they'd have sent a pro. Yet Nathan's death bore none of the hallmarks of a mob hit. On the other hand, if word got out that Morris had taken a payoff, his career would be over, and he'd face serious prison time. A prosecutor would be familiar with police procedure and know how not to leave any evidence. Yes, he was the likely culprit, but how would he have identified Nathan, given the dark street? And tracked him down? Must've followed him home that night.

He could produce no proof sufficient to convince the detectives to suspect the DA of murder. What about bribery? Since he took one bribe, no doubt, he had accepted more. That was the way to put the officers on Morris's trail. After his arrest, they might find evidence to connect him with the homicide.

Nathan hovered above Lt. Hanrahan's desk. When the lieutenant got up and went for coffee, Nathan swooped down and punched keys on the cop's computer. A photo of Heather Morris, Scott's beautiful blonde wife, standing next to a BMW in front of their million-dollar home, popped onto the screen.

The lieutenant returned with a Styrofoam cup and took a seat. "How'd this get here?"

Detective Lopez glanced up. "What?"

"This picture."

"I have no idea."

As Hanrahan studied the screen, Nathan focused intense concentration on one thought. *How can Scott Morris afford a veritable mansion, luxury cars, and a trophy wife on a public servant's salary?*

"Lopez, I believe the universe is trying to tell me something. Our illustrious prosecutor is living beyond his means. Have you seen his wife? Looks like a fashion model or movie star. I'll bet she's high maintenance. Didn't he grow up poor and work his way through law school?"

"That's right. It was part of his campaign when he ran for District Attorney."

"We'd better look into this. He might even be connected to the Rafferty murder, but I can't see how."

Nathan hung around headquarters for three days while Hanrahan and company investigated the prosecutor's finances.

"Lopez, Marchetti, we've got enough to have a chat with Mr. Morris." The lieutenant logged off his computer and rubbed his hands together. "He's reported no income beyond his salary for the last five years, and his wife hasn't worked since their marriage. There's no legitimate way they can afford their house or the cars they drive. Plus, he insisted on handling the Cappucci case himself, and it isn't going as well as expected. Might be throwing it. It's after six. He oughtta be home by now. Let's go."

Wow! This was it. Still, Nathan needed to beat the authorities to the Morris place. They didn't have probable cause for a search warrant. To nail the corrupt official for murder, he'd have to figure out a way to make it happen.

Moments later, he zoomed through the wall of the DA's residence. Scott sat in his study, glass in hand, a bottle of Glenfiddich single malt at his elbow.

Outside the window, an unmarked police vehicle pulled to a stop. Time for Nathan to reveal himself. He materialized in human form right in front of his murderer. "Hello. Remember me?"

Scott did a double take, his face in an incredulous stare. "It can't be."

"But it is. I'm here, and I remembered, at last, what I saw that night—you taking a bribe from Niccolò Cappucci. You shot me because you feared I'd tell what I knew. The irony is that you'd have gotten away with it if you hadn't. I didn't realize what I'd seen until I retraced my steps afterward. Now, you're doomed."

"I don't think so." He pulled a handgun out of a drawer in the side table and fired, but the bullet passed through Nathan without effect. Scott's jaw dropped. He emptied the magazine.

"You're wasting your time. You already murdered me. I'm a ghost. Now, you're done for." He rendered himself invisible.

The front door crashed open. All three detectives rushed in.

Morris rambled. "He's gone...thank goodness...I've killed him, this time for certain."

Hanrahan stepped forward. "What's this?" He took the gun from the soon-to-be-former DA's hand. "A 9-mil Beretta." He glanced at his companions. "Want to bet that it matches the bullet that knocked off Nathan Rafferty?"

Both remained silent.

The lieutenant grinned. "A sure thing. Once we secure our search warrant, I suspect we'll also find evidence that he took bribes. Get this creep out of here. For now, we can hold him for discharging a firearm in the city limits."

Warmth spread through Nathan. With this resolved, he could move on.

A golden staircase materialized, a bright light at the top. With a broad grin, he began his ascent.

Clothes Do Make the Man

Upstate New York, 1948

Brandi shook her head. "Why do I put myself through this?" She wriggled and tugged as she squeezed into the too-tight gold sequined costume designed to showcase her figure and display her long, shapely legs. A necessary, if distasteful, requirement that enabled her to serve her primary function in *Arthur Howard's Illusions Extraordinaire* — to distract the audience.

As she wrestled the top over her shoulders, the door banged open, and in rushed her employer. "It's gone. I don't—"

Both hands raised, Brandi shouted, "Stop right there!"

He skidded to a halt.

She crossed her arms and glared at him. "Arthur Howard, you may be the boss but that gives you no right to barge into a girl's dressing room unannounced."

His face flushed. "Sorry, I was so upset I didn't take time to think." He reversed course.

"No need to leave. You're here now. Might as well make yourself useful and zip me while you tell me what's the matter." She turned her back to him.

With difficulty, he wrenched the zipper from waist to neck, inch by inch. "This thing's tight. Have you gained a few pounds?"

"It's always been snug, and never you mind how much I weigh." *Confound it!* The first indication that he'd paid her the least bit of attention, and he'd called her fat. The dope. "Now, tell me what brought you charging into my dressing room minutes before showtime."

"Right. What a disaster. My suit.... It's gone. Vanished. The hat, too."

She attempted to hold back a giggle.

"This is no time to laugh." He tugged at his collar. "It's serious. I've never performed in anything but my custom-designed tux."

"You have to admit it's funny. Somebody made a magician's outfit disappear." Brandi took a seat at her dressing table and checked her platinum blonde Veronica Lake hairdo in the faded mirror. She nodded. Sultry and eye-catching, just the way Arthur liked it.

"I fail to see any humor in the situation." He paced across the room, all ten feet of it. "What am I going to do?"

She turned on the stool to face him. "As they say on Broadway, 'The show must go on.'"

"Without my suit?" He ran a jerky hand through his hair. "I'm not sure I can."

"You have to." She stood, stepped close, and captured his eyes with hers. "The theater has sold hundreds of tickets. If you don't go on, you may never perform in a decent venue again."

He extended his hands out at his sides. "What'll I wear?"

She fingered his lapel. "The navy pinstripe you have on will do fine."

Eyes downcast, he mumbled, "I'm not certain my magic will work without my tailor-made tuxedo."

"What you wear shouldn't affect your skill. Your act's mere illusion, after all."

For a moment, an expression flashed across his face that she couldn't interpret, as if he held some secret she wouldn't understand.

With a smile, she grasped his forearm and guided him toward the door. "Go on back to your dressing room. Take deep breaths, and compose yourself. You've got this."

"Now, folks, meet my assistant, the bodacious Brandi."

As she strutted from the wings, he stepped forward and said in a stage whisper, "What guy wouldn't want to take a sip of that?"

Guffaws broke out throughout the half-full theater accompanied by scattered catcalls and whistles.

Brandi stifled a groan. The indignities a girl had to suffer to keep a job now that the boys had come home after the war. She pasted the usual smile on her face and swayed her body as she turned to face the audience.

The first twenty minutes of their performance passed without incident. Arthur managed to pull thirty feet of multicolored silk out of an apparently empty hand, and the card tricks worked as planned. He stuck numerous swords through a box after Brandi climbed in, and when he opened it, she stood inside unharmed. Then, the white dove disappeared into the false bottom of his birdcage when she covered it, and Arthur waved a magic wand over it. At least, the thief, or whoever, hadn't taken it, too. She bit back a grin as she imagined him fluttering his fingers over the illusion instead.

But when he lowered the wand and pointed it at the cage to make the bird reappear, a bunch of posies popped out of the end, and the feathered fowl remained hidden. Arthur turned toward the audience, his mouth agape and a dazed look on his face. The crowd must have accepted it as part of the act, for laughter rippled across the theater and everyone clapped.

By the time the applause died down, he'd recovered his composure. When Arthur glanced at Brandi, she handed him a battered top hat.

He whispered, "Where did you find this?"

"In a box of old props backstage."

"Way to go. It might work, thanks." With a forced smile, he faced the audience. "Watch as I pull a rabbit out of this hat."

He set the topper upside down on a table, waved his hand above it, then reached inside. And pulled out...a bunch of carrots. Arthur stood motionless, his eyes glazed over.

After a moment, Brandy announced, "It seems our cottontail has vacated the premises. I'd say he's out to lunch, but it looks like he's left it behind."

The audience roared.

Arthur maintained his fake smile through the rest of the performance, but when the curtain fell, he dashed away. Brandi followed but failed to catch him. Just as she stepped through the stage door into the alley and faced the street, he crossed the sidewalk, hailed a passing cab, and hopped in.

Brandi exited the hotel elevator on Arthur's floor. No telling what she'd find. Storing away the props and managing the other post-performance chores had taken her the better part of an hour.

She hurried down the hall toward his room. A radio blared nearby. "...accompanied by daughter Margaret. In other news, today Secretary of State, George C. Marshall, announced the 'Marshall Plan' to provide funds to assist European countries in their recovery from the devastation of World War II. On the local scene—" The broadcast cut off midsentence.

Arthur's door stood ajar. An odor of bourbon poured into the hallway. No need to guess where he'd stopped on the way. After she passed through the doorway, Arthur staggered from the closet and tossed a heap of assorted garments willy-nilly into a suitcase open on the bed.

She marched inside. "What do you think you're doing?"

He startled as if he'd had no idea she was present. "Make me a laughing shtock, will they? No-shirree. I'm gettin' oughtta here."

Brandi intercepted him on his return trip, led him to the bed, and pushed him to a seated position. "You can't do that. You have a contract. We have another performance here in Schenectady tomorrow. Next, we take the night train to Poughkeepsie, where we have three shows scheduled over the weekend. If you default, not only will you be finished as a performer, you'll face lawsuits." She rolled her eyes. Men could be such knuckleheads.

He hung his head and gave a half-hearted shrug. "I guess you're right. It would ruin me. I'll have to grin and bear it. No matter how humiliating." He flopped back on the bed, feet still on the floor. A moment later, loud snores erupted.

Brandi sighed. *What next?*

On her cue, Brandi pranced onto the stage to applause, louder than normal, and scattered wolf whistles. One guy in the front row shouted, "Hubba! Hubba!" *Oh, brother.* Smile fixed in place, she bowed to the audience. Then she faced Arthur, stunning in a gray tweed that complemented the premature silver at his temples.

The act proceeded as usual until Arthur reached out with a flourish. "My magic wand, please."

Brandi picked the requested item up off the table, but when she extended it in his direction, it turned into a feather duster.

Chuckles broke out throughout the theater.

She pulled out the feathers, dropped them to the floor, and handed him the denuded implement.

"I shall now make the dove reappear. Brandi..."

She lowered a black cloth cover over the birdcage.

When Arthur cast the wand toward the cage, fishing line flew out from it, across the stage, and into the wings. As he raised his wand and examined the tip, the string retracted until a worn old boot appeared on the end. Arthur shook his head.

Laughter spread throughout the house.

Brandi stepped forward and placed a hand beside her mouth as if sharing a secret. "Now I know where the 'beefsteak'"—she made air quotes—"he fed me tonight came from."

Crimson flowed into Arthur's face.

The crowd went wild.

The Friday night show in Poughkeepsie differed little from the last two until Brandi pranced onto the stage with a top hat in her hands. She stifled a grin as she handed it to Arthur, who set it upside down on a table. "I will now pull a rabbit out of this hat." He gazed into the audience, eyes wide. "I hope." He waved his hand above the topper. "Al-a-ka-zaam."

A cobra rose slowly out of the hat, swaying back and forth as if mesmerized by a snake charmer.

Arthur jerked his hand back, strode to a nearby counter, and grabbed his magic wand. A sword shot out from the end. He stared at it, shook his head, and stalked forward with the blade raised high. The viper dropped from view. Eyebrows raised, Arthur glanced at the audience. With exaggerated movements like Sylvester attempting to sneak up on Tweety Bird, he tiptoed toward the hidden critter and circled the table to scattered chuckles. He peeped into the hat, turned to face the crowd, and rubbed his chin. Then, he picked up the hat, punched his fist through it, knocking out the top, and held it up to show everyone it was empty.

Uproarious applause burst out. Arthur took a bow and extended his hand to Brandi, who responded with a curtsey. Still clapping, the audience rose to their feet.

When the curtain fell at the end of the performance, she rushed over to Arthur. "It thrilled me to see you go with the flow tonight. Everybody loved it."

"Figured I might as well ham it up and give them their money's worth, but I can't take the humiliation. After tomorrow night, I'm through. I told my agent to cancel the rest of the tour. I'm sorry this puts you out of a job."

"Please, don't quit." Brandi laid a hand on his arm. "Wait here. I'll be back in a minute." She scampered off the stage.

Moments later, she returned with the purloined tux, trousers, and hat in her hands.

His jaw dropped, and he glowered at her through narrowed eyes. "Where did you get those?"

She hung her head. "From the first, I've understood that, at least, part of your magic resided in the suit. So, I took them to force you out of your comfort zone."

The color drained from his face. "How could you betray me this way?" His shoulders drooped. "I trusted you."

Through lowered lashes, she gazed up at him. "I'm sorry. I didn't mean to hurt you. Just wanted you to notice me. To realize I'm more than a pair of legs to distract the audience from your sleight of hand. No doubt, you'll want to replace me after this, but I'll stay on until you find someone else."

His eyes were cold, flat, dead. He took a step back and turned away. "It would be for the best."

Might have known it wouldn't work. Brandi hadn't become a twenty-eight-year-old spinster by having things break her way. She'd blown it, but good this time. After he hired another girl, she'd never see him again, much less get him to appreciate her as a woman. Tears filled her eyes as she shuffled into the wings. How could a man be so blind? She'd done everything she could think of to catch his attention, short of a whack up the side of the head with a two-by-four.

The curtain came down to lackluster applause.

"What a letdown." Arthur's shoulders slumped. "I made a mistake by returning to the old act. The half-hearted response when I performed the same tired tricks doesn't compare to the fervor of the last couple of nights."

Brandi forced a smile. "Don't worry. This was a matinee. Perhaps tonight's audience will be more enthusiastic." *Right...and Tyrone Power will ride in on a white horse and whisk me away to a tropical isle.*

He shook his head. "I doubt it. The act's gone stale. I should have realized it weeks ago from the size of the crowds and the less prestigious venues we've played. The show needs more life. More oomph. The kind we had the last two nights."

Butterflies took flight in her stomach. "You really think so?" Did this mean...? She held her breath.

A grin spread across his face. "Yes, I do. For tonight's show, I'll wear my navy pinstripe, and see what happens."

"That's wonderful." She fanned herself.

"Afterwards, let's take some time off to revamp the act. We'll keep the humor. It adds a great deal to the audience's experience." He stepped nearer and gazed into her eyes. "During today's performance, I took note of all you add. For the first time. Oh, I knew you did your job well, but I remained too focused on my own actions—how I could improve and please the audience." He lowered his gaze. "I'm sorry. I'd never paid attention to how lovely you are. Or taken time to consider your sweet personality...Or how much you've come to mean to me."

He touched her cheek. "You're extraordinary."

Heat spread through her face. "I think you're pretty special, too." Were the dreams she'd held close to her heart about to come true?

"There's one thing I've got to know." He tilted his head to one side. "You have the gift, don't you? You made all those strange things happen."

She studied her shoes as she nodded. "I cannot tell a lie. I do.... and I did."

With a grin, he continued. "Our new format will provide an expanded role for you. You'll still need to wear the sexy costume. It's expected. But how about if I perform a trick and receive a different result than announced, which you make turn out right? Or maybe I'll pull a rabbit out of my hat, then have you take the bunny and change it into something else."

"Do you mean it? You'll make me a real part of your act?"

"I do. We'll even revise what we call the show to include your name, such as *Arthur and Brandi's Illusions Extraordinaire.*" He took both of her hands in his. "And sometime soon, I hope to perform my greatest magic trick of all—to transform you into Mrs. Arthur Howard."

Not What I Wanded

What's that? Gabe Barfield dropped his broom, rushed over near the rear door, and plucked an object off the floor. Black with a three-inch gold tip, the slender rod measured about eighteen inches long. Odd, but cool. In all his seventeen years, he'd never seen anything like this. He carried the item over, laid it next to his windbreaker, and returned to his cleanup duties.

When he finished cleaning the hall, he grabbed his things and headed toward the exit. A poster in the lobby caught his eye. "The Great Zambini—His feats of magic will astound you." A photograph featured a man in a tuxedo who gripped in one hand what looked like the thing Gabe had discovered. If it belonged to a magician, Gabe must have found a magic wand. He held it up. Imagine what he could do with this!

Underneath the picture were the dates April 4-8. Since the show closed last night, The Great Zambini had likely left town. Just in case, Gabe thrust his discovery under his jacket. He didn't want to lose the chance of a lifetime.

The next morning, Gabe strode through the school with a spring in his step.

Dirk Dorffmann, big man on campus and Gabe's number-one tormentor, stepped out in his path. "Hey, Barfbag, where you goin' in such a hurry?"

Gabe sidestepped and continued on his way. He refused to let that creep get him down. Not today. Not when Gabe might have an opportunity to escape Jefferson High's leper colony and be somebody for a change.

Aha! Stunner dead ahead. Angela Devine, head cheerleader and the most beautiful girl in the state, removed a book from her locker. With wavy blonde hair caressing her shoulders, a perfectly-formed oval face, and a figure that wouldn't quit, no wonder she dated the quarterback and had every guy in school panting over her. With her on his arm, Gabe would become the envy of all, and he held the means to achieve this exalted status hidden under the windbreaker draped over his forearm.

From under the jacket, he withdrew the wand. He glanced around. Nobody near her. He raised the rod and lowered it to point in Angela's direction. A flash like a lightning bolt shot from the gold tip toward his dream girl, but before it reached her, a blur crossed in front of Angela, then froze with a shudder as the bolt struck.

He'd done it again. What a loser! He'd even managed to misfire a magic wand, and of all people, instead of Angela, he'd hit Rachel English, the class brain and as much of an outcast as Gabe. To make matters worse, she wore too-large glasses with ultra-dark frames. What a nerdette!

He tucked the item under the windbreaker and bolted around the corner, where he stowed both in his locker before he beat it to homeroom.

Gabe set his tray on an empty table in a remote section of the cafeteria. From his left, Rachel swooped in and grabbed his arm.

"Gabriel Barfield, I've been looking all over for you." She tugged him to face her, flung her arms about his neck, and kissed him smack on the mouth.

Was this girl crazy? He unwound her arms and stepped back. "What brought that on?"

Lips parted, she touched his cheek. "Because I love you, silly."

He gulped as he scanned the lunchroom. Every eye focused on them. Heat flooded his face. Now, he would become more of a laughingstock than before.

Leaving his food on the table, he fled amid a cacophony of laughter and jeers. One voice resounded above all the others—Dirk's. "Barfbag's got an admirer. I can't believe it."

After his final class, Gabe scurried to the restroom. He would hide out in one of the stalls and think, safe from Rachel's constant pestering. He took a seat and rested his chin in his hand.

As best he could determine, Gabe had but one way to avoid permanent pariah status after today's debacle. If he managed to convince Angela to like him, he might have hope. By the time the after-school cheerleader practice ended, Rachel would have left. His last chance to zap Angela.

About four o'clock, Gabe peeked out the washroom door. All clear. He stole through the hall and out to the football field, where he remained hidden in a stairwell until the cheerleaders began to leave. Then he edged out of his hideout and crept closer to Angela's backpack. When all the other girls had gone, she went over to pick it up. From a nearby seat in the first row, he pulled out the magic wand and pointed it in her direction with a flourish as before. This time, nothing happened. No zigzag of light. Nothing at all. He gaped at the useless thing in disbelief.

"Whatcha doin', Barfbag? Directing an orchestra? Ha, ha, ha…"

Gabe whirled around. Behind him stood Dorffmann, who else, clad in his uniform, pads and all. Not only had the magician's tool let him down in his last desperate attempt to cast a spell over Angela, but now his nemesis had seen it all. How humiliating! Could his life get any worse?

The next day, Rachel met him when he arrived at his locker, her eyes bright. She moistened her lips and laid a hand over her heart. "Good morning, darling. I missed you every moment we were apart." She grasped his forearm.

Gag! "Cut it out, Rachel. People are staring."

"So what? Let them gape. I adore you and don't care who knows it." She puckered up and lunged toward him.

Gabe ducked and turned away. *Argh!* How could such good fortune have gone so horribly wrong? He thrust his backpack into the locker, yanked out his books, and scampered down the hall to a chorus of guffaws. He would never live this down. Maybe he should run away and join the gypsies.

A week later, Gabe sat at a table in Starbucks with his head in his hands, an untouched double espresso in front of him. What was he to do? Every day, his leech latched onto him wherever he went. Once, she'd followed him into the guys' restroom. Perhaps he could talk his parents into moving to a different school district. He raised his head and smiled.

Seconds after, his shoulders drooped. Mom loved the new kitchen Dad had remodeled for her birthday, and they'd burned the mortgage two months ago. He shook his head. No way would they agree to move. He was stuck. Limbs too heavy to budge, he stared into his cup.

"Good afternoon, my love." *Her* voice, bright and sunny—and he'd thought things couldn't grow worse. He sat up straight, hands on hips.

With a shove, Rachel moved the table back several inches, plopped onto his lap, and twined her arms around his neck. Her gaze captured his. "I've found you at last. If I didn't know better, I'd think you were avoiding me." Eyes alight, she grinned and fingered a carrot-red curl.

What should he do now? He didn't want to hurt her feelings. After all, it was his fault, in a way, due to his misguided attempt to use that blasted magic wand on Angela, but he dared not lead Rachel on. He must find a way to let her down easy.

"Listen, you can't keep acting this way in public. You're a nice girl—"

"See, I knew you liked me." She gave him a peck on the cheek and hugged him tighter.

Gabe rolled his eyes. So much for letting her down easy. She'd taken the start of what any rational person would recognize as the "It's not you; it's me" get-lost speech and turned it into an endearment. *This is hopeless.*

He stood, pushed back his chair, and backed away from the table. Rachel's hands slid off his neck, and she dropped to the floor, landing on her backside.

After a glance revealed she was uninjured, he sprinted for the exit. As he shoved the door open and stepped outside, he crashed into Brayden Rockland, one of his few friends before this fiasco made him anathema. "Hi, Gabe. What's got you running like a scalded hound?" He peered around Gabe through the glass entry door. "Rachel must be inside."

Gabe sighed. "Too true."

"Dude. Lighten up. Don't worry so much about what people think. In my opinion, you're a lucky guy."

"Are you nuts?" Gabe took a step back. "That wacko's driving me crazy."

Brayden grasped Gabe's arm. "Come on. Let's go somewhere quiet and talk."

He let his friend lead him to the deserted football stadium where they took seats in the bleachers. After several minutes, Gabe broke the silence. "What do you mean, I'm lucky?"

"Duh! To have Rachel like you? She's smart, outgoing, and kind. And if you look past those ridiculous specs, she's cute."

"You don't understand. It's not real." He filled Brayden in on his discovery, his attempt to use it on Angela, and how Rachel had stepped in front of his intended target.

"Aha! That explains it."

Gabe's chest tightened. "What do you mean?"

"Was your plan to have Angela act bonkers over you the way Rachel's doing?"

"Of course not. I only wanted her to like me."

"Just as I thought. The spell would have created normal feelings for you in Angela. But since Rachel already cared for you, her attraction intensified beyond reason when it hit her instead."

Gabe gasped. "What do you mean, she cared for me?"

"She's crushed on you since junior high, but you were oblivious, man. Too worried about what people think about you. She's a sweet girl. You could do a lot worse—such as that airhead, Angela."

He shook his head. "I didn't realize."

"If you wake up and pay attention, see her as she really is, you might like her, too. By the way, do you still have the magic wand?"

"Sure. In my locker at school. Why?"

"I have a way for you to stop Rachel's craziness."

"How?"

"Meet me there first thing tomorrow."

The next morning, Gabe pinned Brayden with his gaze. "Okay, smart guy, what's this brilliant idea to end my nightmare?"

"You'll see. Grab your wand and follow me."

With a glance around, Gabe tucked the source of his trouble underneath his jacket and followed his friend along the hallway. As they rounded the corner, Rachel stood at her open locker.

Brayden grabbed Gabe's arm. "Quick! I'll make sure you have a clear path. Point the magic wand at her the way you did before."

"But—"

"No questions. Just do it."

Gabe brought out the wand, raised it above his head, lowered it, and pointed it at Rachel. A flash of light zigzagged in her direction. She jerked as if all her muscles had clenched at once. Then she turned toward him, and her eyes lit up. "Good morning, Gabe. It's nice to see you."

"You, too." He pivoted toward where Brayden stood. "What just happened?"

"You've reversed the spell. Returned her to the way she was before, when she liked you, but without the obsession."

"Thanks, man. I owe you."

"Yeah, you do. Now, give Rachel a chance. Go talk to her."

Gabe clapped his friend on the back, pivoted, and strode over to Rachel's locker.

"Uh, Rachel..."

She swirled and met his gaze. A smile spread across her face. "Yes?"

Incredible. Behind those huge glasses were eyes of the deepest blue. The lightest smattering of freckles sprinkled over her cute upturned nose. He cleared his throat. "Um, I'd like to...that is...would it be okay if I walk you to class?"

Her grin grew broader. "I'd be delighted." She slammed her locker door and hooked her arm through his.

Gabe beamed. Maybe the magic wand had worked for him after all.

Up in the Air

Henry Fliegenmann clambered toward his favorite lookout point atop Comanche Ridge. The high promontory jutted out into Redemption Valley, which provided a vast panorama of the Comanche Wells settlement below and the broad basin, as well as the forward slope of the mountains that marked its northern boundary.

He climbed up here every chance he got. He came to think, to contemplate who he was and who he would become. At eighteen, Henry remained unsure of himself and detached, even from his parents. Yet, he couldn't put his finger on what set him apart.

As he reached the summit, his breath caught at the vista's grandeur, although he'd seen it a hundred times before—the green grassland, the treelined serpentine silver ribbon that was Thunder River, a backdrop of gray mountains rising into the sky. This place seeped into his bones. He couldn't imagine living anywhere else. It was the reason he came here—this sense of belonging.

A golden eagle rose from a rocky crag, soared overhead, and glided downward. Magnificent. Majestic.

A crack sounded behind him. Henry tried to turn, but two hands shoved his back and propelled him forward into nothingness. The valley floor a thousand feet below rushed to meet him. His heart pounded. *My life's over almost before it began. I'll never know who I really am.*

If only to extend his life for a second or two, he spread his arms and legs. His rate of descent slowed, more than expected. How strange. The fall might not kill him, after all. About thirty yards above the ground, Henry extended his hands a smidgin and drifted upward. *What happened? This must be a hallucination. Or I'm dead and on my way to heaven.*

He moved his arms farther and zoomed skyward. He adjusted them again and came to rest atop his promontory. *Incredible. Beyond belief. Can this be real? Better find out.*

He took a couple of steps away from the edge, ran forward, and jumped off the outcropping. After he dropped a few feet, he reached out and soared as before. *I'm flying! I can't believe it!*

After about ten minutes, Henry returned to the ridge to ponder his discovery. He'd always known something was different about him. Was this the factor that distinguished him? Made him feel he didn't belong? He would keep it to himself. Tell nobody. If anyone found out, they'd make him even more of an outcast.

When he arrived in town, his cousin Will stood by the hitching post in front of the mercantile, as if he'd waited for him. "Hey, Henry."

"Morning, Will."

"Did anything memorable happen on your daily constitutional?"

Henry's heart quickened. He gulped. *Does he know? How could he?* "Well, I saw a golden eagle up close. Spectacular!"

He searched Will's face for any sign of awareness, but Will just smiled. "I've seen several, but always from a distance. You're fortunate to get as near as you did. For now, better hurry inside. Your dad wants you to make a delivery out to the Oakley place."

"Thanks, Will. See you."

Over the next month, Henry's life went on much as before. Not a bad life, but somewhat off-kilter, more so since his discovery. *What ought I do about this thing, this newfound ability? Should I use it, somehow? If I do, everyone will think I'm a freak and belong in a circus.*

One morning, Henry rode out to the Circle M with a special delivery letter for James Montgomery. While on the way, he ruminated about his "situation." As he rounded a curve, movement in the rocks ahead caught his eye. He shaded his eyes and searched the hillside. Nothing in sight. *Did a head pop up? Could somebody have hidden amongst those boulders? If so, they're bound to be up to no good.*

Henry pulled his mount to a stop behind a boulder alongside the road. What should he do? What *could* he do? He checked the sun. *It's nearly noon. The stage from Canyon City ought to come along soon. I have to do something.*

He did his best to find an alternative, without success. He had no choice. He would have to use his—what might one call it?—gift. Or curse? He had no other way to discover in time what was going on. He dismounted and tied Roscoe to a snag. *Although I've flown off a cliff, can I take off from the ground? I have to try.*

Henry ran toward town. Once he reached top speed, he leaned forward and stretched out his hands. His feet lifted off, and he made a gradual ascent. He circled behind the ridge to remain concealed from anyone who might have hidden on the opposite slope.

He landed near the pinnacle of the rise and picked his way up and over the crest, in search of a vantage point from which he could look down into those rocks unseen, but with such rugged terrain, he had to creep halfway down to reach a scraggly bush that clung to the hillside. He parted its branches and gazed down at the area where he'd spotted movement. Sure enough, five rough-looking men hid there. One face a familiar one, from a wanted poster at the sheriff's office—Matt Ballinger, leader of the notorious Ballinger Gang.

Henry climbed stealthily toward the summit and glanced skyward. *It's past noon. I'd better hurry. The stage should arrive any minute.* He ran along the ridge out of view of the outlaws and took flight. He sailed a half mile up the road before he landed. Then, he hoofed it in the direction of Canyon City.

Moments later, dust rose in the distance. Within ten minutes, the stagecoach crested the nearest rise. He stepped to the center of the roadway, waved his hands above his head, and yelled, "Stop!"

As the conveyance drew nearer, it slowed for an instant. Then the driver cracked his whip and snapped the reins. The horses surged forward and bore down on Henry. His heart jumped into his throat. With no time to run, he leaped instead and lit behind the fast-moving vehicle. He ran in pursuit, flew into the air, swooped downward, and landed on top of the coach.

"Driver, you need to pull up!"

"How'd you get back there?"

"Never mind. Stop, now! Matt Ballinger and his band of outlaws are lying in wait round the next bend."

"Why should I believe you? I don't know you from Adam."

"I'm Henry Fliegenmann. My dad runs the general store in Comanche Wells. I'm unarmed. Look around. There's no place to hide within a thousand yards. What have you got to lose?"

"Okay, you win." The driver tugged on the reins and engaged the brake.

When the coach came to rest, he turned to Henry. "What do you suggest? I have to reach Comanche Wells and beyond."

"I hadn't thought that far ahead." Henry stroked his chin. "Hmm. Backtrack about a mile and turn right onto an old wagon trail. It comes out on the Dalton road a couple of miles from town. It's rough and will take longer, but it sure beats a shootout with the Ballingers."

"I'll do it. But if you've steered me wrong—"

"It's true." Henry crossed his heart. "I swear. I'll ride along to show you the way."

"How did you get out here anyhow?"

"I left my horse up yonder beyond where I spotted the outlaws."

Late that afternoon, the stagecoach limped into Comanche Wells and pulled to a stop at the Wells Fargo depot. "Thanks, son. I have no idea what I'd have done without your help."

"Think nothing of it. Now, I need to talk to the sheriff."

Henry raced off down the street toward the sheriff's office.

"Henry! Where's your horse? Why did you come in on the stage? That entered town from the wrong direction?"

He slowed to a walk but kept moving. "Sorry, Dad. No time for conversation. Got to tell Sheriff Jones something important." He accelerated, again.

"Henry! Come back here!"

He opened the door and rushed in. A deputy sat with his feet on the desk. "Where's the sheriff? I need to speak to him right away."

"He left a while ago to make his rounds. Said he planned to stop at Mabel's for supper before he returns. I'd help you find him, but I can't leave my prisoner."

"No problem. Thanks,"

Henry dashed across the street to Mabel's Restaurant. A bell jingled as he entered. Um-um, fresh bread. His stomach rumbled. Sure enough, the lawman occupied a table near the rear, with a coffee cup in his hand and an empty plate on the table in front of him. Breathless, Henry rushed to him.

"What has you in such a lather, boy?"

"I spotted the Ballinger Gang about noon out by Rocky Bluff, waiting to ambush the Canyon City stage. Hurry. You might still find them nearby."

"Noon?" He stood. "And you waited this long to tell me? Did the stagecoach make it through?"

"That's why I got here this late. I flagged it down and guided the driver into town by the old wagon trail. He and his passengers are somewhat shaken, but well."

"I'll round up a posse. Maybe we'll get lucky. There's a $500.00 reward for Ballinger? If I catch him, it's yours."

The potential for such a windfall should have excited Henry, but he hung his head as he trudged down the street to the mercantile. He'd failed to complete the mission Dad gave him and been abrupt, if not rude, to Dad. What punishment would his father have in store for him? With luck, he would only have to "volunteer" to muck out stalls at the livery for a month. But what if Dad discovered his secret?

Henry walked through the doorway. His father scowled at an open ledger. "Dad, I'm sorry—"

"Son, are you all right?" His father dashed to him. "It's all over Comanche Wells what you did. Everybody says you're a hero."

"I'm no hero. I did nothing more than anyone would in the same situation." He bit his lip. "Dad, I didn't deliver Mr. Montgomery's letter."

"I'm sure he'll understand under the circumstances. We'll take it to him first thing tomorrow. Where is it?"

"In my saddlebags. I left Roscoe tied up five miles from town. If I find somebody to take me out there, I can still ride out to his ranch today."

"Not a chance. You wouldn't make it back until long after dark. It's not safe with those desperados at large. Tomorrow's soon enough, but you ought to retrieve your horse before nightfall. Will's around someplace. I'm sure he'll drive you."

After a couple of months, the hoopla over Henry's rescue of the stagecoach and the subsequent capture of the Ballinger Gang died down. Although the other people his age no longer made fun of him, he still seemed a man apart, exacerbated by his struggle with what to do about his recently-discovered "gift." He'd kept his secret and hadn't flown since the incident.

What should he do? He'd gone over it a thousand times with no resolution. He needed advice. From someone he could trust. A person who wouldn't consider him a candidate for the asylum. Who would keep his confidence? *Will—the logical choice. He's more like a brother than a cousin.*

Henry found Will down by the river. "Do you want to come with me to my special place?"

"What a privilege! You want me to go along?"

"Enough of that, smarty pants. I need to talk to you about something important, but to make certain nobody overhears."

"Sure. Let's go."

Once they reached the peak, Henry chose a rock where he could survey the valley and urged Will toward another nearby. "I have something to tell you, but you have to promise you won't tell anyone."

Will raised his right hand. "I promise."

"Several months ago, someone pushed me off the cliff."

"Oh? And you're here to tell it?"

"You'll think I'm a lunatic."

"No, I won't. Go on."

"I didn't die, because I can fly."

Will laughed. "At last."

Henry's brows raised. "What? I don't understand your reaction."

"You've finally accepted your destiny."

"What do you mean?"

"*I* pushed you."

"You what?"

"Your father urged me to do it. See, you had never figured out your true identity. Therefore, we had to give you a shove."

"But I can fly."

Will shrugged. "Sure you can. I can, too, as can my dad and yours. It's part of our heritage. How do you think we got our name—Fliegenmann?"

"I know it's German, but I don't speak German."

"It means 'flying man.' We live quiet lives, but whenever we have an opportunity to use our gift to help others, we do. Now, you're one of us, for real. You used it to save the stagecoach, didn't you?"

"Yes."

"Your father will be thrilled that you've embraced your legacy. You must tell him."

"I will."

The next morning, Henry again visited his overlook to reflect on the previous day's events. He'd tossed and turned all night but had yet to recover from the shock of Will's revelation. Everyone born a Fliegenmann had the ability to fly. No wonder he felt disconnected from others, but since he accepted his true lot in life, he no longer needed to hold back. He could be himself.

He took a seat on a rock, content just to be and to scan the lush valley. *What was that? A buckboard moving fast.* It missed the curve, left the road, and sped toward the river. The horses must have run away.

After a brief running start, he leaped into the air and zoomed after the speeding conveyance. *How can I stop them and not scare the driver to death or reveal my secret? There's a tree ahead. Perhaps I can use it.*

Henry alighted near the treetop. He descended to a low-hanging branch and waited. As the carriage passed under him, he dropped onto the back of the lead animal. He grabbed the harness and pulled the team to a halt mere yards from the steep riverbank.

He hopped off and hurried to the buckboard. The driver's displaced bonnet concealed her face. When he took her hand, warmth raced up his arm and into his heart. She stepped down and removed the headgear.

Sarah Montgomery! Henry's cheeks grew warm.

"Oh, Henry! I was terrified. And you saved me. You're that kind of man. No wonder I've had a crush on you since school." She twined her arms around his neck and pulled him toward her. As their lips met, he went weak in the knees. Had she not held onto him, he would have fallen.

Perhaps his gift wasn't a bad thing, after all. "Sarah, how would you feel about having kids who can fly?"

The Wizard of Farrlen

As the sun rose over Mount Thurlam, casting a golden glow on the village of Farrlen, Paragoni stepped out of the thatched-roofed cottage he called home and beheld the beauty of his homeland. Nestled between rolling forested hills, the hamlet sat on the banks of the silvery River Turvois. Could anywhere in the universe be more beautiful? More tranquil?

A terrific roar echoed through the valley. A smoke cloud obscured Pinnacle Peak to the west. He shuddered as Kael tottered up beside him, leaning heavily on his cane.

"Master, with the splendor of the sunrise, I had forgotten our peril." Paragoni turned toward the south end of the dusty main street, where charred remains of a half-dozen huts marred the landscape.

"Understandable, my son. A characteristic of youth. One you'll be loath to lose as you mature."

"What will we do if the dragon returns? Our people might not escape harm a second time. The creature may wipe out the entire village. How can we defend ourselves?"

His mentor's shoulders drooped. "The answer lies beyond my ken. My powers have proved inadequate to stop him, but we must find a way. The only action I can take is to spend time in solitary prayer and ask the gods for help. I shall withdraw into my cave ere nightfall."

At the sound of voices and footsteps, Paragoni whirled around. The village chief approached with five townsmen behind him. "Kael, I have recruited our most valiant warriors to slay the dragon. Each has won countless victories over both man and beast. We have come to seek your blessing on their quest as the resident wizard."

"Nay, I cannot give it. You dispatch them on a suicide mission. This dragon is too powerful."

"They must go, regardless. Our situation is perilous beyond measure. We have to do something ere we all perish. Godspeed, men."

They turned and marched toward the dragon's lair.

"**M**aster, the warriors have not returned after three days. What does this portend?"

The wizened wizard folded his hands in his lap. "As I predicted, they have met their fate."

"No doubt, their families worry about them."

"True." Kael nodded. "Let us go out and retrieve any remains. This will help their loved ones find closure as they grieve. Pack needed supplies. We shall be gone all day."

After Paragoni gathered food and drink, he tossed the sack over one shoulder and joined his mentor. "Ready, Master."

The old wizard led the way down the street and up into the mountains. Although he stopped to rest on occasion, he never seemed to need to get his bearings.

As the shadows lengthened, Kael halted in a glade. "This is the place. Search well."

Paragoni examined every inch of the clearing and found naught but five piles of cinders, each not more than half a span in diameter. As he gazed down at them, his master joined him. "Not much to remain of brave men, is it?"

Kael's head jerked up. "Come, we must hasten. The dragon approaches."

They scooped up the remains and set out for Farrlen as fast as the older man could move. After several minutes, he paused behind a bush and peered between the branches. Paragoni did the same.

The leviathan stood where they had been moments before. A fearsome beast, indeed. At least twenty cubits from head to tail and with smoke shooting from its nostrils. The creature turned from side to side as if searching for something. As it faced south, Kael nodded.

Paragoni opened his mouth to speak, but when the older man placed a finger to his lips, he remained silent.

The wise man crept away, Paragoni at his heels.

When they had distanced themselves from their nemesis, Paragoni whispered, "Why did you nod earlier?"

"I recognized the dragon. Did you take note of the scar on his neck?"

"Aye."

"I did that. Many years ago, I served as an apprentice wizard, like you, in a land far away. A band of dragons attacked the town. My master and I went out to meet them. He possessed powers much greater than mine and slew four of the creatures before Ignis, the elder of the two that remained, overcame him. I managed to kill that dragon and inflict a severe wound on Infernoth, the younger one. Because of his youth, I made the mistake of letting him live." Kael sighed.

"Later, I journeyed to Farrlen and settled there. Infernoth must have searched for me all these years. Now, he's found me and desires to avenge his father's death. To add to my suffering, I believe he plans to destroy the village and all its inhabitants before he kills me."

Kael's chin sank to his chest. "Somehow, over the years, Infernoth's power has increased to epic proportions. It will take a miracle to save us, for I cannot."

Paragoni's throat ached. If only he could do something to comfort his master. But if a wizard of Kael's wisdom and skill could not cope with this dragon, Farrlen was doomed. His muscles went weak.

The wise man straightened and squared his shoulders. "Come. Let us return home. I must spend more time in prayer. Deliverance by the gods is our sole means of survival."

P aragoni trudged down Farrlen's principal thoroughfare and surveyed the destruction wrought by Infernoth's forays into the village. His arms hung limp at his sides. Was all lost? More than a quarter of the settlement lay in ruins with two dozen men, women, and children slain. Many villagers wandered aimlessly. Their glazed eyes stared at nothing.

Near the chief's cottage, he stopped. The chief and his nephew, Malachus, stood in the road with Kael. The wizard pumped his fist up and down. "Stop this insanity. You have sent out two other emissaries. Neither has returned. To send a third will not result in a more favorable outcome. Why sacrifice another young—"

The chief raised a hand. "I've heard your thoughts before. However, we face dire conditions. We're running out of food. My people have eaten neither meat nor bread for a week."

Kael shook his head. "We have an ample stock of beans from last year's bumper crop. Nary a soul will starve."

"Silence! I have made my decision. Malachus will travel over the mountain to Dimmire and purchase the needed supplies."

Kael mumbled under his breath as he limped away.

Paragoni rushed to catch up. "What now, Master?"

"I shall return to my cave and commune further with the gods."

"Mayhap Malachus will succeed where others have failed."

Kael sighed. "Nay, he has no more prospect of success than of making an axe head float in the River Turvois."

Bloodcurdling screams arose from beyond the village.

Tears filled the old man's eyes. "Infernoth must be killing him slowly to terrorize the villagers." The old wizard shuffled off toward his place of prayer.

Paragoni clutched his arms against his chest. Did they have any chance to survive when faced with such a fearsome adversary? He turned and made his way homeward.

An hour later, the ground trembled, and a clatter arose to the south. He stepped outside.

A young boy ran up to him. "My father sent me to fetch Kael."

"He's in his cave and left orders not to disturb him."

The child grabbed Paragoni's arm. "Then, *you* have to come. While my sister played amidst the ruins, the earth opened and swallowed her."

"Lead the way."

The youth raced down the street with Paragoni close behind.

When they stopped, two dozen villagers lined the edges of a huge hole. Paragoni gazed into it. Dirt, stones, and debris from burned-out houses lay piled up twenty cubits below. No sign of the missing girl. "The roof of a cave must have collapsed. Mayhap the child rolled out of sight when she fell. I need to go down there. Fetch me a rope."

A middle-aged man rushed away and returned a moment later. He handed Paragoni a length of rope.

"Tie it on that rock." He pointed to a large stone nearby.

With the rope secured, he climbed down hand over hand. When he reached the bottom, he scrambled off the debris and surveyed his surroundings. A dark passage led off to one side and likely extended beyond the rubble in the opposite direction.

He picked up a cubit-length branch off the pile, grasped one end, and touched his finger to the other. It burst into flame, an instant torch.

He held the light high as he advanced into the cave. The girl lay still about ten strides from where he'd descended. He secured the torch in a pile of stones, then bent over and tapped her shoulder. "Lyra, awake."

Her eyes fluttered open.

"My leg, it hurts. She reached toward her left leg, which protruded at an unnatural angle."

"It's broken. Let's fix you up, shall we?" He grasped the injured member above and below the break and recited a healing incantation. Nothing happened. He repeated the action with different words. Still no change. He scratched his head. "I'm sorry. I cannot heal you, but take heart. Kael will make your leg whole again. Let's get you out of here."

As he reached for her, she pointed over his shoulder. "Look!" He turned. A rolled-up scroll stood on a stone shelf. What could it be? "You have the eyes of an eagle."

She blushed at the highest of all compliments.

He carried the girl to the opening and looped the rope under her arms. "Pull her up, but take care. She's injured."

While others lifted the girl, Paragoni hurried to the shelf, retrieved the scroll, and returned as the rope dropped again through the hole. He tied it around himself. "Ready."

At the top, he rushed to her. By this time, Kael had arrived and bent over her. He removed the splint, stroked the injured limb, and recited the same incantation Paragoni had first used. "Arise, child."

She stood and ran into her mother's arms.

Paragoni narrowed his eyes. "Master, why did I fail to heal her?"

Kael touched his arm. "My son, you doubt your abilities. You must overcome this to become my successor." He lowered his gaze. "What do you have there?"

"An ancient scroll. From the cave." Paragoni held it out.

The old man took it and unrolled one side about a cubit. "It's the scroll of Arteris, lost centuries ago. My grandfather spoke of it whilst he trained me. I must study this."

The next day, Paragoni arose to find Kael's bed empty. He located the old man outside, seated on the ground with the scroll on his lap.

"Good morning, Master."

"Aye, 'Tis the best morn in weeks. Cast your eyes on this." He passed the scroll to Paragoni.

After a moment, Paragoni looked up, a huge smile on his face. "The ancients discovered that Mordren crystal has the power to control fire. If only we could acquire some."

"According to the scroll, it comes from a cave near the top of Pinnacle Peak."

Paragoni spoke through clenched teeth. "Might as well be on the moon, for Infernoth has made it his lair."

"Since obtaining this mineral is our one hope of survival, we must find a way to distract the dragon, sneak into the cave, and return with the crystal."

"But how?"

"I know not. Come, let us consult the village elders."

Soon, Paragoni stood behind Kael while the wise one related what he'd learned to the chief and four older men seated in a semicircle. "We have to lure the monster away from the mountaintop."

The chief leaned forward. "Someone can attract his attention, whilst you two take another route. Mayhap a feigned attempt to go for supplies."

The old wizard sighed. "Certain death for the one who goes."

"Aye, but a necessary sacrifice of *one* to save scores. I shall take this action myself. I have sent too many others to their deaths."

Paragoni spoke for the first time. "But you are chief. The villagers need you."

"Kael will appoint a new leader when you've saved Farrlen."

"When do we act?"

"The day is young. Why not now?" The chief's lips pressed into a firm line.

Kael stepped forward. "No reason to delay, but first, we two must gather tools and supplies."

Half an hour later, they met the chief outside his house. He set his feet in a wide stance and thrust his shoulders back. "Let's do this. May the gods bless thee." With that, he led two donkeys southward, on the road to Dimmire.

With a glance skyward, Kael turned to the north. Paragoni hefted a bulky sack over his shoulder and hurried to catch his mentor.

Once out of view of Farrlen, the wizards circled toward Pinnacle Peak. If their luck held, the chief would have attracted Infernoth's notice and lured him far enough away for them to remain undetected.

Moments later, a scream of agony echoed in the distance. Paragoni stopped and whirled. A cloud of smoke rose about a mile away. *Looks like the chief caught the dragon's attention.*

"Let us make haste. Infernoth may return now to his lair." The ancient one stepped out faster than he'd moved in years.

Soon after midday, the two crested the peak and located the cave. Kael paused at the entrance. "Hand me a torch."

Paragoni pulled two out of his sack and handed one to his master, who touched it with the tip of his finger. The torch erupted in flames. Paragoni followed his mentor's example with the same result.

The wise one led the way inside the cave. About fifty paces inside, a wall of a greenish crystalline substance glowed in the firelight, the Mordren crystal.

Paragoni removed a hammer and chisel from the sack and set to work. Within the hour, he had cut free a dozen good-sized chunks. Kael gathered them, inserted them into two small leather pouches, and passed one to Paragoni.

"Leave everything else. We must travel light." The old wizard headed out the entrance.

Before they traveled far, a clatter occurred up ahead. Kael halted. "Let us separate. You go right. I shall go left. Mayhap one of us will survive."

Seconds later, the dragon stepped out in front of Paragoni. He dived to one side as flames shot from its mouth. And missed.

Kael shouted, "Let him go! It's me you want!"

Infernoth turned. Fire burst from his mouth and consumed Kael. A smoke cloud arose along with the stench of burnt flesh.

Paragoni pulled out the pouch and removed the largest crystal. He couldn't fail again as he had with Lyra's broken leg. The entire village's survival depended on him. He dared not doubt himself any longer. He held out the crystal toward Infernoth and began an incantation.

The dragon spun his way. Flames gushed forth, but as Paragoni spoke the last word, the fire flickered and died. Infernoth's head drooped as he slinked away vanquished, his power destroyed.

Paragoni had overcome his self-doubt. He dropped to his knees. "Fare thee well, Kael. I shall do my best to serve Farrlen as wizard."

Best-Laid Plans

Kevin ushered his beautiful, statuesque blonde date into the bistro. Aromas of pasta, tomatoes, and garlic filled the air. Dishes clattered. Silver scraped against china.

As the hostess led the way to their table, Kevin scanned the room. With red-and-white-checked tablecloths, vermilion tile floors, and greenery, the homey neighborhood eatery hardly qualified as one of the trendy upscale restaurants Alexandra favored. But Giuseppe's featured the best Italian food in Kansas City.

Uh-oh. Bogey at two o'clock. A former high school teammate sat nearby with two cronies, all about half-drunk. Three sets of eyes followed Alexandra as they passed. No surprise there. With her heart-shaped face, golden shoulder-length hair, and Angelina Jolie figure enhanced by a black body-hugging cocktail dress, no wonder Joe and his buddies ogled her.

Joe pulled his tongue back into his mouth long enough to speak. "Wow, Kev. What a hottie!"

Kevin glared, but said nothing as he passed. At least, no baseball fans had recognized him, as far as he could tell.

He smiled and pulled out her chair. "Honey, do you remember this place?"

She glanced around her. "Should I?"

He sat across from her. "We came here on our first date. Occupied this same table."

"Oh, right." Her lower lip protruded. "But I had my heart set on Eddie V's."

"I chose Giuseppe's for a reason." Kevin fought to keep a straight face. "I forgot something. Be right back." As he dashed toward the street, a huge grin broke out. Wouldn't she be surprised? No more veiled protests about his choice of eateries.

From his car's trunk, he pulled a supersized bouquet of Mylar balloons. Some bore pictures of hearts. Others read, "I love you." The largest asked, "Will you marry me?"

Next, he opened a jeweler's box and removed a two-carat emerald-cut diamond ring. He tied it to the balloons' string, slammed the trunk, and rushed inside.

Kevin crept to a place about thirty feet from their table and stooped behind a potted plant. He'd spent two hours with Mama Rosa earlier, making sure everything was perfect for this once-in-a-lifetime event.

With her help, he'd tested wind currents to identify the one place from which the balloons would fly directly to Alexandra when released. Right here, by this ficus. Nothing could go wrong.

From the corner of his eye, he spotted Joe and the other two Stooges staring at him. Just his luck to choose a vantage point ten feet from those bozos.

Kevin blocked them from his mind and focused on the task at hand. He spread the branches and peered through the gap.

She sat facing him, gaze fixed toward the entrance. Lips pursed, she fingered her emerald necklace, his gift last Christmas.

When the aisle cleared, Kevin freed the balloons. The ring would hang at table height when it reached her if all went as rehearsed. She'd be ecstatic.

He stood and watched. Halfway there, the balloons reversed direction, although a breeze still cooled the back of his neck. How could they travel against the wind?

As a professional athlete, he'd surely catch them when they glided past, the way he might snag a line drive. But the parcel drifted beyond the three dolts, out of reach unless Kevin dived across their table. One dolt stretched toward the bouquet and bumped the table. A full glass of ice water tumbled into Joe's lap. He jumped up amidst a string of profanity. A trio of girls at the next table gasped, pointed, and laughed. It looked like he'd wet himself.

Kevin chuckled in spite of his desperate situation, then watched, helpless, as the balloons passed above a greenery-topped partition. *Rats!*

When Kevin rounded the divider into a separate dining area nearer the entrance, his quarry hovered near the ceiling. With luck, he would retrieve everything with no harm done.

A second later, the balloons dipped, and the ring landed in the lap of a young woman seated alone. He took a step toward her.

Oh, no! His mouth went dry. Oval face framed by light brown curls. Indigo eyes. Why was Erin Kelly here? A Harrisonville girl, born and bred, she seldom made the forty-mile drive into the city.

Perhaps, if he cut his losses, he could escape unnoticed. Before he moved a muscle, she turned and faced him. *Too late.* Her face lit up like the fireworks after the Royals' Fourth of July game. His stomach roiled. Now he was in for it. He trudged toward her on leaden feet.

With a broad grin, she leaped to her feet as he reached her table. "Oh, Kevin. Yes! Of course, I'll marry you." She untied the ring and slid it onto her finger. "I'm so happy. And stunned. I've loved you forever, but never suspected that you love me, too. I haven't seen you since the All-Star break. You—"

"Erin, I—"

"—set this whole thing up. What a clever ruse. To get me here for a blind date who'd stand me up. I don't remember telling you I'd registered on YourPerfectMatch.com. Oh, I love you with all my heart." She threw her arms around his neck, raised on tiptoe, and kissed him full on the lips.

Warmth flooded Kevin's body. His breath quickened. His fingers tingled until he circled her waist, drew her closer, and deepened the kiss. *Whew!* If he'd had any idea she harbored such latent passion, he might have considered her more than a next-door neighbor and friend. A jock and big man on campus, he'd traveled in different circles at school from the bookworm and computer nerd.

At length, she ended the embrace and returned to her seat. "We have loads to discuss."

Struggling to catch his breath, he nodded and dropped into the chair nearest to her. Boy, did they need to talk. What a mess. Why, oh why, had he come up with the outlandish balloon proposal?

He leaned forward, propped his elbows on the table, and placed his chin in his hands. *Dear God, what now?*

"Sweetheart, this will thrill our parents. Mom adores you. Told me as a teenager I ought to try harder to attract your attention, but I prayed you'd choose me because you wanted to, not because I set out to trap you." She hugged herself. "It's a dream come true."

In her excitement, Erin must not have noticed Kevin's hesitancy. He shook his head. How did he get himself into such muddles? Her words faded as he zoned out.

Later, Kevin struggled to his feet. "I have to use the restroom." He hurried off. Once out of Erin's view, he slowed and caught his breath. Engaged to Erin Kelly. *Phew!* To tell her the truth would devastate her. She'd loved him for years, while he remained clueless. The last thing he wanted to do was to hurt his oldest and dearest friend, but would it be right to marry her when he'd intended to propose to someone else? What a tangle!

He swallowed the lump in his throat and slogged toward the men's room. Maybe if he washed his face, he would regain sufficient composure to think.

"Just where do you think you're going?" Alexandra screeched.

He'd forgotten all about her. How much time had passed? Half an hour? He gulped and executed a slow turn. Arms crossed, she stood by the chair where he left her.

Might as well face the music. He took hesitant steps in her direction. "Sorry, I—"

"You bring me to this dump, then leave me all alone, starving." She stamped her foot. "I'll not stand such treatment. I'm through. Understand? Through."

"I'm sorry. It's—"

"I really don't give a—" She added a series of epithets inconsistent with the usual veneer of sophistication she projected. "The Chief's quarterback has urged me to date him. I'll do it. *He* respects me." With a huff, she breezed past and out of sight.

So much for their whirlwind romance. He wiped his brow. What a narrow escape. From the start, he'd had an inkling Alexandra cared more about the lifestyle he could provide her as the first baseman for the Kansas City Royals than for him, but he had denied it because of her beauty and apparent affection for him. Tonight, she'd revealed her true colors. Come to think of it, the assistant to the team's owner had paid him little attention until he signed a seven-year, sixty-million-dollar contract.

Now, what about Erin? He sighed. Best hurry to the washroom or become a liar on top of everything else. Then he'd talk to her. *Lord, I need help here.*

When he emerged, he received no flash of insight, no message from on high. Perhaps, God figured Kevin had gotten himself into this mess without consulting Him and would have to handle the predicament absent divine assistance.

When he plodded past the partition into Erin's line of vision, she stood, still holding the balloons. Unlike Alexandra's anger and impatience, her broad smile welcomed him. A sudden realization struck him like a Justin Verlander fastball to the ribs. He hadn't looked at Erin in years. Not really. To him, she remained the chubby girl with thick glasses of his youth, but she had changed. Cute rather than beautiful, she'd exchanged the spectacles for contacts. Although not as busty or thin as the Barbie-doll build now in vogue, her figure must attract considerable male attention.

He sat next to her and took her hand. "Erin—"

Her eyes glistened as she met his gaze. "How marvelous! I still can't believe it. I've loved you for ages, but I admired you more after you reached the majors. You didn't buy the big, fine house the way many professional athletes do. You keep an apartment near Kauffman Stadium but still live with your parents in Harrisonville during the off-season. Of course, maybe I'm just selfish because I can see you more often."

"You? Selfish? Never. There's no one more unselfish. You spend hours each month at the church's food bank. Babysit your sister's kids to give her a night out with her husband. Tutor underprivileged children."

Her face turned red. "I didn't realize you knew all that."

"You've been my closest friend forever. I know almost everything about you. You're the most wonderful person I know." His heart raced. Why hadn't he recognized it sooner?

She beamed. "I had no idea you cared about me as I do about you. In fact, I thought you were dating a fashion model."

"Alexandra may look like a model, but she's a Royals' employee. It didn't work out."

"Say, didn't I see her dash out of here a while ago?" The color drained from Erin's face. One hand clutched her chest. "You brought her here, didn't you?" The string slipped from her fingers. Balloons floated toward the exit until the string caught on a rubber tree plant.

Kevin gulped. Now what? He couldn't deny it, but didn't want to hurt her.

"This is all a mistake. It's her ring, isn't it?" She grabbed it and twisted, but the band refused to budge. Tears streamed down her cheeks. She covered her face with her hands.

Now what? He'd broken her heart. Which shattered his. He scooted his chair closer and wrapped his arm around her. "Dearest Erin, I'm so sorry. I wouldn't hurt you for the world, but I have to come clean. I did bring Alexandra here to ask her to marry me. A monumental blunder."

Bile rose in his throat. "The balloons were supposed to carry the ring to her, but it went to you, instead. Against the air currents. Maybe somebody's trying to tell me something. Sometimes, it takes a baseball bat to the noggin to knock sense into a guy's head, to help him see what's right in front of him."

Erin raised her head and gazed at him, eyes tear-filled.

"Now that I think of it, Alexandra wouldn't have cared for this ring. Not flashy enough. It's unpretentious but lovely, like you. Your beauty radiates from the inside out."

Eyes wide, she clasped her hands under her chin, as if in prayer.

"What a dunce! I didn't have sufficient self-awareness to grasp how much I love you. I should have asked for your hand ages ago." He bent down on one knee and took her hand. "Erin Kelly, you'll make me the happiest man on earth if you agree to be my wife."

Eyes alight, she nodded. "Yes, I will. If you're sure I'm not your second choice?"

Standing, he drew her to her feet. "Never. You're the one I've always wanted, but I didn't have sense enough to realize it. What could be better than to marry your dearest friend?"

He gathered her into his arms and lowered his lips to hers. When her fervor matched his, Kevin's heart raced. At length, he pulled away and gazed into those fabulous indigo eyes. "We'll buy you another ring tomorrow."

"Oh, no you don't. I love this one. Besides, after all that's happened, something tells me I'm supposed to have it."

The string slid free from the potted plant. The balloons rose toward the ceiling. One bobbed up and down. "*Well, Marilee, our work here is done.*"

"I agree. What a brilliant idea, Howard, to loosen Randolph's plug, so the escaping air pushed us against the wind."

"Thank you, dear. I'm rather proud of that one."

The door opened. An air current tugged the balloon bouquet out through the doorway where it rose into the sky.

PART IV — HISTORY AS IT NEVER WAS

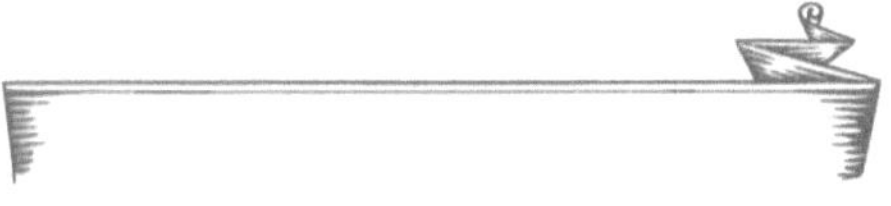

Surprise Attack!

What if the United States had not ignored numerous red flags in 1940-41 that indicated the Japanese would launch a sneak attack against U.S. Naval vessels in the Hawaiian Islands?

Pearl Harbor, 4 December 1941, 1543 hours

"Jacoby! Get in here!"

Lieutenant Reginald Jacoby dropped the daily report on his credenza, rushed into Commander Mulligan's office, and stood at attention in front of his superior's desk. "Sir?"

The brawny senior officer's face glowed red from his graying hair to the always-crisp collar. A sheen of sweat glistened in the light from the window. What had the skipper riled up? Had Reggie messed up somehow?

With jerky movements, the commander held up a folder, eyes alight. "This is it!"

"Sir, what do you mean?" Reggie's breath caught. He must have made a grievous error.

"We've received reports that the Japanese plan some type of sneak attack. Intelligence suggests Pearl Harbor as the target. Oh, at ease, Lieutenant. Sorry about that."

Reggie moved to parade rest. Gooseflesh covered his arms.

"Yesterday, radiomen from a commercial vessel intercepted and recorded coded Jap transmissions in the North Pacific. Radio direction finding fixed an approximate location two hundred miles northwest of Honolulu."

Dozens of butterflies took flight in Reggie's stomach. "Sir, we need to make preparations, ASAP. The offensive may occur at any time!"

A smile deepened the crow's feet at the corners of Mulligan's eyes. "We have a plan, son. But it all depends on you."

Reggie leaned forward and met the commander's gaze. "I'm ready, sir. To do whatever I can." His heart pounded. What would they ask of him? He prayed he'd live up to his bold words.

"Hold your fire, Lieutenant. Officials at the highest level took care to give little credence to the threat—in public—but behind the scenes, our forces have taken steps to lure the Japanese into a trap." He pointed to Reggie's chest. "This is beyond Top Secret."

"Certainly, sir."

Mulligan's hand clenched into a fist. "You understand all our aircraft carriers have left port on various missions?"

"Yes, sir. My friend, Ensign Monroe, is aboard the *Arizona*."

"The operations were a ruse. Those vessels now maintain radio silence in positions away from shipping lanes, north and east of the islands."

Reggie sucked in a quick breath. "Lying in wait?"

"That's right. Within the hour, they will receive coded transmissions with orders to move into position based on this report." Mulligan tapped the folder, which he'd dropped on his desk. "Now, for your part in all this. I'm confident you're the man for the job."

"I appreciate your confidence in me, sir." Reggie's pulse kicked into high gear. "I'll do my best to live up to your expectations."

Commander Mulligan's gaze bored into Reggie's eyes. "You have *two hours* to change into civvies and travel to Ewa Beach, where you will board the *Marlin*, a tuna boat. You'll serve as a spotter. You're well acquainted with the silhouettes of Japanese naval aircraft, are you not?"

"Yes, sir. I've studied them at length."

"The crew consists of actual fishermen. They will fish as usual, except they shall do so at coordinates you give them." Mulligan extended a sealed envelope. "Here are your detailed orders. Don't open them until you're at sea. The captain will follow your directions without question. Have him cruise near the stated position. Use the boat's radio and regular frequency to make your coded report per your written instructions. Any questions?"

"No, sir." Reggie pressed his lips into a firm line.

"Very well. You're dismissed."

"Aye, aye, sir." With a forced smile, Reggie snapped to attention, pivoted, and strode toward the door.

"Wait a moment."

Reggie did an about-face.

"You might need these." The commander bent, opened his bottom drawer, and pulled out a pair of oversized binoculars.

"Right." Reggie stepped forward and took them from Mulligan's hand. "Thank you, sir."

"Best of luck, Lieutenant." He extended his hand. "A great deal depends on the success of your mission."

150 miles NNW of Honolulu, 7 December 1941, 0637 hours

As he'd done from dawn to dusk on the two previous days, Reggie stood near the bow of the *Marlin,* raised his gaze skyward, and rotated 360 degrees at a slow, steady speed. He completed the revolution and then snapped his head to the left. What was that dark blur at ten o'clock? He lifted the binoculars to his eyes and scanned the sky until he focused on the objects he sought. Just as he suspected. Mitsubishi A6Ms, over a hundred of them—he held his position for a moment—as best he could tell, headed due south.

He lowered the binocs and raced to the bridge. "Captain, I need your radio."

"I'll call ahead. The radioman on duty will accommodate you as soon as you can reach the comms shack."

"But first..." Reggie removed the field glasses from around his neck and handed them to the skipper. "Ten o'clock. What do you see?"

The captain raised the binoculars. "Good Lord! Is that what I think it is?"

"I'm afraid so. What's your take on location?"

"Eight miles off the port bow."

"I concur." Reggie raced toward the comms shack, composing the message in his head as he ran.

When he stepped through the hatch into the room, the radioman smiled at him. "I'm Miller. The Skipper called and said to give you access to the radio. What do you need from me?"

Reggie swept his hand in the direction of the communication equipment. "Just make certain this contraption works. I have information vital to naval operations."

"Sure thing." Miller threw a couple of switches and spoke into a microphone. "Honolulu, this is the fishing boat, *Marlin*. Come in, Honolulu."

"This is Honolulu. Go ahead, *Marlin*."

The guy reported the vessel's current geographic coordinates and handed the mic to Reggie, who held it to his mouth and cleared his throat. "This is the daily catch report for the *Marlin*. We landed more than a hundred tuna. We plan to relocate eight miles west today, and then turn south tomorrow. Over."

"Message received. Honolulu out."

"*Marlin* out."

Reggie returned the mic to Miller. "Thanks."

The radioman raised his brows and scratched his temple. "What was all that about?"

After a deep breath, Reggie met the man's gaze. "I reported in excess of a hundred Japanese fighter planes off our port bow headed south."

Miller's eyes grew as wide as signal lamps. "You're kidding?"

"No. It's for real." Reggie placed a hand on the radioman's shoulder. "Don't worry. We're ready for them."

Pearl Harbor, 7 December, 1941, 1324 hours

Back in uniform, Reggie jumped out of his jeep and sprinted into headquarters, bound for Commander Mulligan's office. He slowed to a fast walk once inside the building, but skidded to a stop when he encountered his superior in the hallway. "Sir, how did it go?"

He slapped Reggie on the back. "Better than expected. Well done, my boy, well done. Your report enabled two of our carriers to launch their airplanes. They intercepted the Japanese en route. Our navy fighters stopped one-third of the strike force and delayed the rest. Their success, coupled with your early warning, gave us time to move all our ships out of port and disperse them. We lost one battleship and another sustained heavy damage, but between their guns, land-based antiaircraft batteries, and Army Air Corps fighter planes from Hickam Field, our forces shot down another twenty Jap aircraft."

Reggie slumped against the wall and glanced skyward. "Thank God, we anticipated the attack."

Mulligan nodded. "True. Otherwise, they might have destroyed almost the entire Pacific Fleet, but I saved the best news for last. We sent the *California* north two days ago. With the position data you provided, her new radar detection system identified the precise location of the hostile task force. The remaining carriers launched a counterattack while the Japanese planes were away. Aided by *California's* fourteen-inch guns, our fighters sank one enemy carrier, crippled the other, and dealt heavy casualties to additional vessels in the convoy. When their aircraft returned, they had no place to land."

Reggie stood erect, shoulders back. "Sir, thank you for the opportunity to participate in this mission."

"You earned it. I placed the full report of damage inflicted on the enemy on your desk. Suffice it to say, we've severely diminished their ability to launch additional attacks. We've prevented massive amounts of death and destruction. For one thing, Jap ships bound for the Philippines earlier have reversed course."

"Are we at war?"

"No. At least, not yet. President Roosevelt addressed the nation on the radio two hours ago. He's ordered all Japan's diplomats out of the country and called Congress into special session. He'll address a joint session tomorrow. If we do declare war, with Japanese forces depleted and ours close to full strength, I suspect they'll sue for peace within the week."

Reggie's pulse accelerated. "Wonderful news! Now, if we have to fight Hitler and Mussolini, we won't have to wage a two-front war."

"Speaking of the European situation, I have new orders for you." Mulligan grinned and handed him a stack of printed papers. "You report to the Threat Assessment Desk at the Pentagon two weeks from today, Lieutenant *Commander* Jacoby."

Previously published in
White County Creative Writers Anthology 2018

Transatlantic Union

What if the breakaway American colonies had lost our Revolutionary War?

"Not only did the War Between the States claim the lives of six hundred thousand soldiers and two hundred thousand civilians, the effects of the evil institution of slavery cause racial strife today, a century and a half later."

While teacher Augustus Thomson droned on, Logan Ahrens leaned over and whispered to Makayla Ellis. "Mr. Thomson sure gets wound up on this subject, doesn't he?"

"And why not? His ancestors were slaves. I think it's horrible what happened and how divided we still are."

"Well, duh."

When the room fell silent, Logan faced the front. Mr. Thomson glared at him. "Logan, do you have something to say more important than the lesson?"

Logan studied his hands. "No, sir."

"Then, I shall continue. Please, pay attention."

Logan sighed. How embarrassing, but at least Grouchy Gus hadn't insisted they share what they'd said with the class.

Logan walked home alongside Makayla in silence. Odd. She always had something to say.

After a while, he said, "What's up? Are you okay?"

She nodded as she met his gaze. "What Mr. Thomson said about race relations. It's a shame people can't get along because of things that happened ages ago."

"Yeah. If only someone could go back and put a stop to slavery before it became entrenched. If we'd ended it without a war, our country might not be so divided."

She snorted, one of her less-endearing habits. "You do realize that's impossible, don't you?"

Arms crossed, he stepped back. "Of course. I'm not a complete moron."

"Sorry, I didn't mean to insult you."

"It's okay." He smiled. "I forgive you. Yet, it *would* be wonderful if it were possible."

They continued to stroll side by side, Makayla with furrowed brow. After a few minutes, Logan broke the silence. "Still trying to solve all the country's problems?"

"Nope, thinking about Mr. Thomson's lesson. I wish we could find a way to help."

Logan stopped, hands stretched out on both sides. "What can *we* do? We're kids."

"I don't know. Perhaps we'll think of something."

He slowed and glanced to one side. "Say, Makayla, how long have we walked home along this street?"

"Four years. Since you moved here in second grade."

"That's what I thought." He pointed to the left. "Have you ever seen that hill before? There. In the vacant lot."

"Not that I recall, but I pay little attention. We're usually talking."

"You mean *you're* usually talking." He grinned.

She thrust her fists onto her hips. "Well, if you think I talk too much, you don't have to walk with me."

"Don't get all huffy. I only wanted to find out if I could get you riled up. It worked, too. Seriously, I enjoy listening to you. You have such strong opinions about everything."

"Ha, ha." She didn't crack a smile. "Now that you've had your fun, why did you call my attention to a hill?"

"It's strange. I scan our surroundings while I listen to you—"

There went those fists to her hips again. She opened her mouth.

"Don't get your feelings hurt. That wasn't an insult. I'm just trying to explain something weird. In all the times we've passed here, I've never noticed this particular hill. And I *have* looked."

Her eyes narrowed. "I'm sure there's a reasonable explanation."

"Maybe so, but I see a cave, and something inside me insists I must investigate."

"It's your natural inquisitiveness. You are a *boy*."

"When's the last time I went exploring? I'm more into computer games. Yet I feel a powerful pull to explore the cave."

"Oh, well. If we have to. Come on. Let's go satisfy your curiosity."

Moments later, the two stood outside the cave's entrance. Although they stooped to enter, it opened into a sizeable chamber.

Makayla stepped to the center and whirled around. "This is amazing. How can this room fit inside such a small hill? It's at least twenty feet across and fifteen feet high."

"Beat's me. Everything about this is bizarre. I wonder if there's more to this place."

"Look." She pointed. "To the right."

"A passage. Let's find out where it goes."

"If you insist."

Logan clicked on his phone's flashlight app and darted through the opening into the passageway, Makayla at his heels. About twelve paces in, the corridor sloped downward. He halted.

She stopped next to him. "What do you think?"

"Let's keep going. We have plenty of room to walk beside each other, and the ceiling's high enough we won't need to stoop."

"Okay. Let's do it."

As they legged it through the cave for a good fifteen minutes, he kept a sharp eye on their surroundings. The tunnel maintained a uniform distance between rough gray rock walls. Unlike most caves, which varied in size from place to place.

"Logan, I think I spotted a glimmer of light ahead."

"Must be another way out." He held out his hand.

By tacit consent, they rushed hand-in-hand toward the glow. Both covered their eyes as they stepped out into dazzling sunlight.

When his eyes adjusted, Logan dropped Makayla's hand and scanned the landscape. Twenty minutes earlier, they'd been on the outskirts of their small hometown. Now, they stood in the countryside. Plowed fields intermingled with wooded areas and grassy pastures dotted with cattle. Where were they?

He turned to Makayla. "Do you have any idea where we are? This doesn't look familiar."

"To me either."

He glanced at his phone. "No service. Maybe we oughtta go back." He whirled around and sucked in a quick breath. "Where'd the cave go? Do you see it?"

She grabbed his arm. "No, but it has to be here." A hand flew to her chest and her eyes widened.

After an hour's fruitless search, he stopped, shoulders slumped. Disordered thoughts ping-ponged through his mind. This made no sense. He scratched his cheek. "Well, that didn't work. We'd better try to find someone to help us."

She clutched the locket she wore every day. "I guess so. It's all we can do."

He took her hand again, and they hiked away from the afternoon sun. After about an hour, they happened upon a dirt road.

Logan bent and examined the roadway. "The packed surface indicates that it's used often. We ought to follow this trail. It must go somewhere."

Sometime later, they entered a forest.

"Halt! Who goes there?"

Makayla and Logan froze.

Makayla's hand trembled in his. Or was it his own hand shaking? His heartbeat raced. Could they find someplace to hide?

Two men stepped out from opposite sides of the pathway. Angled across their chests, each held a long gun that resembled pictures of flintlock muskets.

Logan turned his head toward Makayla. Their eyes met. Who were these guys? The youths faced the men, who must have been on their way to a costume party or reenactment. Their uniforms consisted of blue knee-length cutaway coats over white trousers and vests, along with black tricorn hats.

"Hi, I'm Logan and this is—"

The taller one lowered his weapon, his gaze focused on Logan. "What are you children doing here?"

"We got lost on our way home from school."

The short, plump man turned to his companion. "It would behoove us to take them in hand and report this. We cannot take a chance that word of our position will reach the redcoats."

"Methinks you are correct."

An hour or so later, the two soldiers led their captives to a gentleman who stood with his back to them. Although dressed in similar military apparel, this one wore a powdered wig and sported a saber at his hip.

The taller soldier said, "General, I beg your pardon."

The bewigged gent turned to face the speaker.

Logan's heart leapt into his throat. He struggled to draw a breath. The man before them matched the image of George Washington on the one-dollar bill.

"What is it, corporal?"

"Sir, we found the children in the wood. We brought them along lest word of our whereabouts reach Howe's Lobster Backs."

"I daresay it's too late for that. Our sentries spied a British patrol atop yon hill,"—he pointed to his right — "two hours ago. Our patrols report redcoats taking up positions to our front and on both flanks."

"Regardless, we delivered these two to you. We thought you would know what to do with them."

The general scrutinized Logan. "Young man, pray tell, what do you have to say for yourself?"

"Um..." This couldn't be happening. George Washington had addressed him. What did one say to a man who'd been dead for over two hundred years?

Makayla stepped forward with her shoulders back, chin high, and hands clasped behind her. "General Washington, we are from the future, and we'd like to talk to you about the problems caused by slavery."

"The future? Preposterous. Despite your unconventional attire and peculiar accent." With crossed arms, he stared at her. "Who sent you?"

"No one. We took something of a detour on our way home from school and became lost. We wandered around looking for help until your soldiers dragged us here. Where is here, by the way?"

"This is my camp in Brooklyn Heights. On Long Island."

Logan's mouth dropped open. "Long Island, New York?"

"By all means. Where did you think you were?"

"We live in Laurel, Maryland."

"Maryland colony is many leagues from here. Who brought you?"

"Nobody. As Makayla said, we lost our way after school and wound up here. I don't understand it."

Makayla laid her hand on Logan's shoulder. "It's okay. I've got this." She smiled and turned to their host. "General Washington, I have a question for you. What is today's date?"

"The twenty-seventh day of August in the Year of our Lord, 1776."

Logan's head jerked back. He stared straight ahead, seeing nothing. "But...but..."

With a quick step forward, Makayla snapped her fingers in front of his face. "Logan!"

He shook his head.

"Welcome back to earth." She clasped her hands against her chest. "Don't you understand what's happened? We wished we could do something about slavery's impact on our society. Somehow, our wish has been granted. We've passed through a time warp...or something. Anyhow, we're back at the time of the American Revolution with an opportunity to talk to the Father of Our Country about the evils of slavery. Perhaps we can make a difference. Change history."

"I'm not sure about that. This all seems too weird. It can't be real. Must be a hallucination." Arms out, he did a slow three-sixty.

"Ouch!" He rubbed his side and glared at Makayla. "Why'd you pinch me?"

"To let you know you're awake. This is no illusion. I can't make sense of it either, but I refuse to waste this opportunity."

"Whatever..."

She faced their host. "Sir, please excuse the interruption. My friend here is overwhelmed by what has happened. As I said earlier, we live in the future, the year 2025. Our nation fought a bloody war from 1861 to 1865, after which slavery was abolished. Yet, more than a hundred and fifty years later, the institution's adverse effects persist. We have considerable racial unrest."

"What balderdash!"

"I understand your doubts, General. Time travel seems farfetched, but I assure you it's true. As a slaveholder, I'm sure you question my ideas about the morality of involuntary servitude."

"On the contrary, I have worked with Thomas Jefferson and others to end slavery in Virginia. I would have freed my slaves, but current law prohibits it."

"No kidding?" Logan said. "They didn't teach us that in school."

"Nevertheless, I'm not certain I can help you."

Makayla planted her feet in a wide stance. "Yet, it's so important."

Washington frowned. "Alas, I fear that this fledgling union will rip asunder if we attempt to abolish the practice at this time. We are but a loose confederation of sovereign states. The southern members would withdraw at the first mention of such a proposal, and our coalition would disintegrate."

After a couple of hours of engaging discussion, an officer approached. "Begging your pardon, sir. The redcoats are moving to our rear. If we don't act soon, we'll have no avenue of retreat."

"Cunningham, fetch the men who brought these children to me and make certain they are returned. I don't want them here when the British attack."

He saluted. "Yes, sir." He turned to the youths. "Follow me, please."

The corporal ceased his progress down the dirt road and scanned the surroundings. "Children, this appears to be the place where I stopped you. You should be safe now. Private Durham and I must return to our post. I trust you shall manage to find your way back from here." After an about-face, the soldiers quick-marched toward their camp.

Logan stared at the ground. "Now what? We were lost when they found us, and we're still lost now."

"Beyond question, our brilliant plan to search for someone to take us home won't work, since we're trapped in a past century. We will have to stumble across a route to the cave ourselves."

"Makes sense, I guess." He surveyed the area. "But we failed to locate it minutes after we came out. Why do you think we'll have better luck this time?"

"A different perspective may help." She offered her hand. "Shall we go?"

After a moment's hesitation, Logan took her hand and strolled with her down the lane. They'd walked a hundred yards or less when he came to an abrupt halt and waved toward the right. "That looks like the stand of trees outside the cave, and it has a cliff behind it. I'll bet it's the place. Come on. Let's check."

"I'm positive we'd followed this road for at least a mile before the soldiers stopped us. How can this be the same cave?"

"You ask that when we've traveled two centuries back in time?"

"When you put it that way, my skepticism does seem trivial. Might as well give it a try."

They left the well-defined track, crossed a grass-covered meadow, and rounded the wooded area. Sure enough, the mouth of a cavern yawned in the cliffside.

Logan tugged her hand. "This is it. Let's go."

Makayla didn't budge. "Many caves look alike. How can we be certain it's the right one?"

While he pondered her question, he gazed at the ground. A short distance away, something gleamed in the sunlight. He dropped her hand, trotted a few steps, and bent over. "It's a cellphone. Just like mine." He reached for his back pocket. Empty. When he pressed his thumb to the bottom of the phone, it came to life. "It *is* mine. This has to be the place. Still no service."

He clicked the flashlight app as they entered the cave. Ten minutes later, they emerged back in Laurel. Together they scanned the familiar surroundings.

A huge grin spread across Makayla's face. "We had an incredible adventure, but I'm glad to be home."

"Me, too."

As one, they sprinted down the sidewalk until they reached Makayla's house. She took a step up the walkway but turned back. "I don't think we should tell anyone what happened. Nobody will believe it. It's too fantastic."

"True, they'll think we're crazy."

He nodded. "That's for sure. See you tomorrow."

"Yeah, see yah."

Logan turned and walked next door. Once inside his house, he hurried into the kitchen for a snack. When he dropped his phone on the table, the time lit up—3:20. *Unbelievable. Only ten minutes later than when they'd left school. Most days, it took fifteen to walk home.*

"**A**s we have studied, tomorrow we celebrate the anniversary of the most important event in our nation's history."

Logan leaned toward Makayla. "Our adventures yesterday didn't change Mr. Thomson any."

"Nope. But what's he talking about? Tomorrow's May sixteenth. What happened on May sixteenth?"

Logan shrugged and tuned in again to the teacher.

"Have a wonderful Union Day, everyone."

Logan and Makayla glanced at each other. Her brow furrowed. She mouthed, "Union Day?"

The bell rang.

Once outside, she met Logan's gaze. "Have you ever heard of Union Day?"

He shook his head. "Never." He pulled out his phone and opened it. "Google, what's Union Day?"

"On May 16, 1846, representatives of Great Britain and its American colonies signed an agreement to form the Transatlantic Union. Since that time, the two entities have functioned as one nation governed by a single body of laws. The Union Covenant serves as a constitution upon which subsequent statutes are judged."

Logan glanced at Makayla. "I've never learned anything about this. Sounds like we never won our independence. Let me google the Revolutionary War."

He typed in the requisite information and clicked on the first result. "Wow! It says the American colonies' abortive attempt to gain independence from Britain ended in August of 1776 when British troops surrounded Washington's colonial army on Long Island and forced a surrender."

"Amazing. I remember reading where Washington retreated across the East River to Manhattan. What happened?"

He shrugged. "We must have delayed Washington long enough that he lost his opportunity to escape."

"This would explain the strange flag in the classroom."

"What flag?"

"I couldn't make it out, but I'm positive it wasn't the Stars and Stripes."

Logan held his phone out to her. "Did it resemble this?"

"I think so. The Union Jack was in the upper left corner, and those hands clasped over squiggly lines look like what I saw."

"The article says it represents a union of two peoples separated by an ocean."

Makayla scratched her head. "I wonder what effect this had on slavery."

He input the necessary information. "Parliament abolished the slave trade throughout the British Empire in 1807 and the practice of slavery in 1833."

Her eyes glowed. "I can't believe it. We changed history. America didn't have to fight a war to free the slaves. Just think of the impact on race relations—and all because we went exploring on the way home from school."

"Yeah." He smiled. "And wanted to make a difference."

PART V — FLASH FICTION BONUS

Zikes! There's a Fungus Among Us

Zike-L sighed. To her right, her mate, Zike-R, still snoozed. Soon, Danny would arrive, slip his feet into them, and off they'd run. A huge grin had crossed the boy's face when he opened the shoe box last month and ran his fingers along the sleek Z and cool racing stripe on her side.

As she gazed across the locker room, a dozen strange organisms approached, their progress relentless. Each consisted of a stack of six irregular spheroids inside a gelatinous substance.

She hopped down from Danny's cubby. "Who are you? Why are you here?"

The leader stopped in front of her. "I'm Tinea Pedis, here on a mission."

Zike-L scratched her heel with one lace. "I won't let you give Danny athlete's foot!"

"You can't stop us. We've got you outnumbered." He leaped onto her toe and motioned toward his fellows. "Come on, gang, climb aboard."

She eyed adjacent cubbies. "Beerok, Off-Balance, help me!"

Both pairs of colleagues replied to her in unison, "Go away, don't bother us."

She jumped and twisted. The intruder dropped to the floor and lay motionless. Then she stomped each of the others and dusted off her laces. "That takes care of them."

The leader croaked, "That's what you think. We're only the scouts. Look behind you."

Zike-L pivoted. Legions of fungi marched inexorably toward her.

Zike-R hopped down beside her, yawning. "What's happening?"

Before she could respond, the first invaders attacked. Despite her best efforts, they swarmed over and inside both her and her sidekick. *How can I save Danny?*

She surveyed the room. On a nearby table sat a can of antifungal powder. She hopped over and kicked the table leg until the container tipped. A cloud of protection enveloped both Zikes.

As the shriveled fungi staggered away, one coughed out, "Whoever invented this stuff should be fungalated."

Zike-L followed them to the door. "Don't come back, or I'll give you more of the same."

As she turned, the clock on the wall caught her attention. "Ten o'clock. Danny will be here any minute." She hopped across the room and onto the shelf with her tongue hanging out. *What a day!*

The door burst open and two dozen boys, Danny included, streamed in to dress for gym class.

About the Author

Gary L. Breezeel began his first novel in 1964. That blight on the literary world remains unfinished to the everlasting benefit of readers everywhere. However, he has completed drafts of two Christian romance novels. Neither is ready for publication. A member of American Christian Fiction Writers, he has written short stories in various genres, including mystery, romance, fantasy, and horror. He has won numerous contests including Del Garrett's Gimme the Creeps Contest, White County Creative Writers' Contest, and Del Garrett's Triple Scoop Writing Contest. A native of Southeast Missouri, Gary now lives in Searcy, Arkansas.

About the Publisher

The Little Red Writing Hood is an independent publisher committed to helping talented local writers share great stories.